4/7/06.

IN THE NAME OF
SISTERHOOD

Ethel!
Be Blessed 3 Enjoy

Author: Phyllis Simms

Phyllis Simms
"Puerto Rico 06"

In The Name of Sisterhood

The Cataloging-in-Publication Data for this title to be supplied by the Library of Congress.

ISBN: 0-9760810-0-8

EAN: 978-0976-08100-5

Copyright: Txu993-410

Cover Design by Phyllis Simms and Sal Gaetan

Layout Design by Rebecca Simmons

Printed by Morris Publishing
3212 East Highway 30
Kearney, NE 68847
1-800-650-7888

Acknowledgements

First and foremost, all praises to my Lord and Savior Jesus Christ. I am truly thankful for being blessed with the ability to create uplifting stories through the power of words.

Thank you William Akin III for all of your encouragement and determination in seeing this book published. You believed in this novel from the beginning and refused to let me give up. Thank you for introducing me to my wonderful Editor and mentor Mrs. Rebecca Simmons author of "Nobody's Business." Rebecca, your enthusiasm and keen eye is what I needed in order to bring this book to fruition. Thank you for all of your guidance and support.

To my parents Jonah & Rever Simms, whom I love beyond words and life itself, thank you both for encouraging me to follow my dreams and to never give up.

To my sisters Sylvia, Lynette, & sister/cousin Chakela, Life's funny isn't it? In the end it's really all about love... You three are my foundation. ☺

Also, much love to my brothers Sammy, Rufus and Corey... We are all unique because of one.

Many thanks and love to my second father Lemuel Darnell Taylor ("AKA" Tetley)

Aunt Mildred, my other mother, thank you for a lifetime of laughs and sincere encouragement to... *Go on girl and just do it!* I love you aunty...

Aunt Helen, thank you for your generous heart and sincere advice, you are truly wisdom! To my Aunt Bessie & *Godmother*, you are truly a blessing to the entire Cross family, thank you aunty for encouraging me to not worry about other folks and to just follow my dreams.

Speaking of the Cross family, Aunt Annie, Aunt Gail, Uncle Bay, Uncle James, Uncle Biggie and Uncle Zan, much love to you all. And to my male cousins, aka "The Cross crew" David Barnell Cross, & Steve Cross you two guys are the best! Kevin, Keith, Glen, Guy, David, Darryl, Hose, Jamie, Stacy, Kenny, Calvin and Michael Cross, Kevin Miller, Ricky Butler, Craig Johnson, Victor & Ricky Richardson, you know I love you guys...especially Warren Bryson, thank you cuz for being my constant chauffeur to Brooklyn. Without you, I could not have made it. ☺

To the Ladies... aka "The female Cross crew" Lisa Cross, Diane Anderson, Clarice Miller, Crystal Johnson, Yvonne Jones, Carlie Cross, Sonya Cross, Sharon Richardson, Mary Young, Theresa Scott, Mary Higgs. Thanks Cousins for all of your love and support! Grand-pop (RIP) would be proud!

And to the Simms side of my family... I will never forget our summers in North Carolina which is a story in itself for we were all blessed to be cut from the same cloth and loved by our Grandparents (RIP) Arabella and Festus Simms.

Aunt Lula and Uncle Junnie Kirkland, thank you both for always being there, I love you both so very much. Also much love to Aunt Melvina (Toot) and Uncle Tommy, Uncle Steve and Aunt Louise, Aunt Betty and Uncle Hodgess, Uncle James (Beat) and Aunt Edna.

Many thanks and love to my cousins: Dexter Simms, Reverend Jeffery Simms, Darvis Simms, Michael Simms, Larry Simms, Derrick Simms, Paul, Festus and Niece, Angie Simms, Deborah Simms, Cynthia Brown, Sharon McFall, Patricia (pinky), Towanda, & Joyce... Eva, Renee, Yvonne & Patsy aka the Hodgess women... (Gifted with brains as well as beauty, your creative talents forever amaze me!)

Many thanks to my extended Family: Aunty Phyllis from Bermuda...Thirty some-odd years ago God blessed you and my mom to meet by chance on an airplane ride from Bermuda. Because of you Aunty, she is alive and well today. I love you so very much and Uncle Barnell too.

Much love to my #1 brother in-law Wendell Gumbs, and to my beautiful sister in-law Rhonda Hines Simms, thank you for loving my brother Sammy... he's the best right! Mrs. Wilhelmina Gumbs, thank you for all of your advice and support and for stepping in and not giving up until the contracts were signed.

Mr. George Gumbs, Yes I really do know the answer!☺ Thank you Wanda Gumbs Sims for being one of my original readers, your enthusiasm was greatly appreciated. Thank you Sean Miller...little brother and author of (A Gambit for love) for all of your support and for introducing me to Sal. Sal thank you for bringing my book-cover to life.

To my true sisterhood friends Beverly Williams Johnson and Jackie McArthur-Farmer, I will never forget our days at Norfolk State! Speaking of Norfolk State, thank you Curtis Bunn for all of your encouragement in getting this project off of the ground, your novels Baggage Check and Book Club were great!

A special thank you to my Apostolic Family... too many to name, but I love you all, Especially Mother Macpherson, Barbara Cotton, Brenda Page, Linda Lawrence, Dena Calhoun, Jackie Conyers, Sarah Yancy and my beautiful cousin Monica Jones Reed. Alvin Wayne Thomas, yes you are truly my brother, thank you for always looking out for me. Vicky Vanessa Thomas, for you a lifetime of love, I am forever your sister. BOS and LD, there are no words to describe the love and admiration I feel for you both...

Thank you JR Ramos... My Latino brother ☺ Lisa Ramos, Myra Lorenzano, Shapran Simmons and Tonya Suttles for all of your support. Shay Robinson and Sherri Simms; thank you both for keeping my hair in perfect condition and a special thank you to Linda of Va. where *Hair Graphics* started it all.

Sharon Hopson thank you for helping me get back into shape. Your classes are amazing!

Last but not least, to my island Crew! Sharon Osborne, you were there from the beginning listening when no one else would. Yes I know. that's what true friends do! Thank you girl for reading my manuscript over and over again, you are truly the best! Thank you Stacy Harden for taking the time to read my manuscript when I know you had much better things to do!☺ Much Wuv to ya...as well as to Melanie, Tootie, Kim, Monique, Karen, Tonya, and Tonja (TC)... Oh my God! Ladies I will never forget St. Thomas and Jamaica... Where we created a lifetime of memories of Fun in the Sun ...What's Next!

Phyllis Simms

In the Name of Sisterhood...

In this life, there are so many learning experiences
that help make you who you are today.
This book characterizes the lives of four women who
developed a bond stronger than blood.
Here, their bond was and is:

IN THE NAME OF SISTERHOOD

"Sisterhood"

WOW!

What a word.

Two words.

One Meaning

Each Word Able to Stand Firmly On its Own

Together...

A Strong Statement

Representing

Strength~ Honesty~Trust~ and~Everlasting Love

A Simple Analysis

Time and time again, we are often plagued by the horrors of today's ever changing world.

We have allowed television programs, talk show hosts, news media and numerous experts to direct our lives, analyze our thoughts and tell us who we are, who we're suppose to be and how we're supposed to act.

Funny but I've always believed, GOD blessed each and every one of us with a mind of our own.

You know, the organism that allows you to think and to decide, to choose and to make choices, to believe and to know.

OUR MINDS
MY MIND
OUR STORY

I HOPE YOU'LL ENJOY IT!!!

One

6:00 Friday Night

As Brandy entered the restaurant you could not help but to notice her. She was absolutely beautiful. Beautiful in a way that said, "Hello world! Here I am!"

Brandy was tall and walked with a stride similar to that of a first prize horse. Head up, back straight and eyes straight ahead. Her body was well toned and could compete with the likes of Angela Basset without breaking a sweat. And she had a smile that said, "Hello" before she uttered a single word.

What was most striking about Brandy was her beautiful flawless chocolate complexion. She was a true Nubian Princess.

"Damn," she quietly mumbled as she looked at her watch. "I can't believe I'm the first one here. It never fails," she sighed. "Whenever we plan a girl's night out, I'm always the first to arrive. It's 6:00," she quietly hissed. "Where are they?"

"May I help you?" the host asked.

"Yes," Brandy answered. "I have a 6:00 dinner reservation for four."

"Oh yes," he said as he checked off her reservation. "Here it is." The host chuckled as he said, "I see you made your dinner reservations three months ago."

"Yes I know," Brandy laughed. "But I had no choice. Between getting on your reservations list, making sure my friends were available and finding a babysitter, it took some time."

"I can only imagine." The host laughed as he motioned and said, "Please, allow me to show you to your table."

As the host escorted Brandy to her table, her mind wandered. It had been three months since Sukenya announced her engagement, and Brandy was looking forward to tonight. "For tonight," she laughed. "Is a night about celebration, a night about believing in a dream and celebrating the outcome with those closest to me. That is, the young women of *yesteryear, and* the true women of today."

The true women so fondly remembered by Brandy were Sukenya, Alexandria and Nicole. Young women *who*, close to twenty years ago, *met* by chance during their freshman year at Norfolk State University and *chose* to become friends.

A friendship of sisterhood!" The young women often laughed, during those ever so wonderful days of meeting new roommates, attending college band camp, and pledging. The days of falling in and out of love, hanging out together at football games, attending college parties, spring rushes and step shows. The days of making late night runs to Hardees, while pulling all-nighters studying for midterms and final exams.

"*A friendship*," Brandy quietly thought as she sat and waited for her friends to arrive. *That has survived the test of time with the same love, trust and respect of true sisters.* "A friendship." She smiled as she inhaled then slowly exhaled as her inner mind recited her theory about sisterhood.

Sisterhood cuts across all walks of life. It doesn't matter where you come from, what your family background is or how you arrived, so long as you arrived. Stronger and more determined than ever, to

15

live the life God truly blessed you with. Without apologizing to anyone for who you were. That is...

A woman...
A woman who had
gone through life's challenges.
Challenges in love,
Challenges in marriage,
Challenges in motherhood,
Challenges in the work place, and
Challenges of death.
But through it all, our bond
could not be broken.
For our bond was created
"In The Name of Sisterhood."

"Brandy to earth," whispered a voice in her ear, first a faint whisper and then laughter.

It was Nicole. "What's up girl!" she laughed.

"What's up?" Brandy asked. "You're late, that's what's up."

"We're not late!" Interrupted Alexandria and Sukenya as they sat down and said in unison. "We're on CP time!"

The ladies choice for the evening was a posh new restaurant owned by one of the hottest businessmen/rappers in New York City. After weeks of trying to acquire reservations, the women all agreed, it was well worth their wait. For the restaurant showcased a mosaic crowd of professionals winding down after a long day at the office. Nurtured by a candle lit ambiance that gave the restaurant a tranquil and serene effect, as a live jazz band enlightened everyone's ears. Laced with a food menu that read like the who's who list of the best Caribbean, Southern and Cajun cuisines throughout the country.

As the women all laughed and mingled, Sukenya exclaimed, "Ladies, let the night begin!"

Sukenya, a beautiful 37-year-old news reporter, is about to marry the man of her dreams. And tonight was her night to celebrate. To celebrate all that she'd dreamed about but never really believed would happen. After all, according to statistics, the possibility of a 37-year-old successful woman walking down the aisle for the very first time was slim to none. Sukenya had, in all accounts, beaten the odds, or had she?

As the evening progressed, the women caught up on one another's latest activities, laughed, reminisced and lost track of time.

"So Nikki, how is the new business going?" Brandy cheerfully asked.

Nicole had recently started her own computer-consulting firm. At 37, she was an absolute computer whiz. Having worked in the corporate world since graduating in 1985 from Norfolk State University, where she earned a dual degree in Computer Science and Economics and graduated at the top of her class. Gifted with brains as well as beauty, Nicole had been through it all. She was the plaintiff of an ongoing lawsuit against her former employer and her marriage had ended in a bitter divorce.

"Business is great!" Nicole answered. "I recently picked up two new contracts and I'm in the final phases of signing another. The Y2K problem had so many companies running scared. My consultants are working night and day! I would love to hire a new consultant. But between attending the court hearings and meeting with potentially new clients, I can't seem to find enough hours in the day. It's exhausting, but it is just what the doctor ordered."

"And!" Alexandria interrupted. "You would not want to disappoint the *Fine Doctor,* would cha now?"

"Alex!" Nicole gasped. "If I've told you once, I've told you a thousand times, he is happily married!!"

"And!" Alexandria laughed in a sarcastic sounding voice and asked. "But is his wife happy?" The entire table fell out laughing.

Alexandria was definitely one of a kind. Beautiful, yet seductive. Funny, but very shrewd. When she was around, anything could happen, and it usually did.

"Yes Alexandria," Nicole answered. "His wife is happily married. Thank you."

"Yeah, yeah, yeah." Alexandria laughed as she waved her hand back and forth and said, "Girl Puhleese. If my doctor was a six foot four, bald headed chocolate replica of the most famous basketball player of all times, why would I care if the brother was married? OK!"

"Alex!" Nicole shrieked. "You have such a one track mind."

Alexandria poked out her lips, rubbed her hips and wiggled in her seat as she replied in a seductive voice, "And ooh wouldn't it be so nice to have your doctor's train running all over my tracks."

"All Aboard," yelled Brandy.

"Choo, Choo," mocked Sukenya as the entire table burst into uncontrollable laughter while they gave each other an agreeable nod backed by high fives.

As the evening ended, they all departed promising to *"get together like this again Sukenya, sometime before your wedding."* The women chuckled as they drove away in separate cars.

Two

6:00 *Saturday Morning*

"Mommy. Mommy. Mommy. Mommy," rang in Brandy's ears. But she did not move. Brandy heard the words again. "Mommy. Mommy. Mommy. Mommy."

This time the words were followed by small giggles and little nudges.

Brandy continued lying in bed listening to their little voices, not yet opening her eyes.
Instead, she silently said a small prayer.

Thank you GOD, for blessing me with such a wonderful and thoughtful husband. Yes! She laughed; Brandy's got a man, a man who loves and appreciates me for who I am, a man who adores our children and understands his role as a father. A man who is: my husband. Their father. My love. Brandy ended her prayer by thanking God for their four beautiful children, (although she'd been pregnant only once). *Fertility Medicine.* Who knew?

Brandy and Darius, her husband of 15 years, had unsuccessfully tried for years to have children, but for some unknown reason, conception seemed impossible. "Relax," Brandy's doctors would often say. "And let Mother Nature take its course." After twelve years, numerous tests and thousands of dollars, Mother Nature never took.

Darius and Brandy were about to give up on the idea when, while vacationing in France, they met a couple who had gone through a similar situation. With the couple's recommendation, Brandy and Darius met with the couple's French fertility doctor. Nine months later, "V*oilà!*" Darius and Brandy were the proud parents of not one, not two, not three, but four healthy babies. Two boys and two girls, Thank you Jesus!

Brandy continued lying in bed as these four little pairs of hands probed her body. First pulling her arms, then gently pinching her cheeks and sitting on her chest while she simply concentrated on their little fingers. *So small*, she thought, *yet so soft.*

"Mommy. Mommy. Mommy. Mommy. We're hungry."

"Can you hear us?" asked one little voice. "We're hungry," the little voice repeated.

"Mommy hears us," replied another little voice as he played with his mother's ears.

"She can see us too!!" the little voice whispered. "I opened her eye. Seeee," he said. As his little fingers held Brandy's right eye open.

Just then, Brandy opened her left eye and said in a funny little voice, "What about me, what about me," while she moved her left eyeball back and forth.

"Aaah!" one of the children screamed, "She's awake! She's awake!"
Brandy was then attacked by a swarm of little hugs and kisses. "Oh well. It's 6:15 am," she laughed, "time to start my day."

As Brandy prepared breakfast for her children, she thought about the wonderful evening she'd had with her "*Sisters*" the previous night and broke into a small chuckle as she said while shaking her head back and forth, "That Alexandria."

"Did you say something mommy?" asked one of the children.

"Oh, no sweetie," she replied. "Mommy was just thinking out loud about Aunty Alex."

"You saw Aunty Alex!" shrieked one of the girls with excitement.

"Yes precious," Brandy answered. "Mommy had dinner with her last night."

"Dinner?" asked one of the boys.

"Mommy I'm hungry." his brother whimpered.

"I know babies, breakfast is almost ready."

"Is Aunty Alex coming over today Mommy?" asked one of the little girls. "Because," she giggled as she stretched out her little arms. "We love her this big."

"She is so funny," the other siblings chimed in as they all began to giggle.

"I know you all love Aunty Alex, and she loves each and every one of my wonderful babies too. But I'm sorry to say, Aunty Alex isn't coming over today."

Just then the phone began to ring. Brandy recognized the number on the caller ID and smiled as she picked up the receiver.

"Good morning Suk."

"Girl, you and that damn caller ID!" Sukenya answered back with a laugh.

"Please," Brandy teased. "My caller ID helps me to keep people like you at arms length."

"Yeah, yeah, yeah," Sukenya laughed. "What Everrr!! Brandy, gurl I have to give you your props

24

for last night because it was definitely one for the books. Wasn't it?"

"Yes it was," Brandy answered. "I was just thinking about that crazy Alexandria before you called."

"Crazy!" Sukenya laughed, "That is an understatement because the girl needs some serious professional help. I'm convinced!"

The two women cracked up laughing.

"Is that Aunty Alex?" asked one of the little girls.

"Oh no sweetie. This is Aunty Suk."

"Aunty Suk!" giggled the other daughter with excitement as she placed her hands up to her mouth and screamed! "We're her flower girls!"

"Is she getting married today Mommy? Is she? they asked in harmony. "Can we speak to Aunty Suk, Mommy" Pleeze?"

"I want to speak to Aunty Suk Mommy," cried one daughter.

"No I want to speak to Aunty Suk," cried the other daughter.

The girls continued going back and forth with their song until Brandy interrupted them.

"Oh no girls," Brandy replied in a sweet motherly tone. "Aunty Suk isn't getting married today. She is however, very busy and say's she will speak with her favorite nieces at another time. She also says she loves all of you very much and asked me to give everyone lots of hugs and kisses. Now please sit down and eat and let mommy finish her conversation."

As the children ate their breakfast, Brandy continued her conversation with Sukenya.

"Sukenya, I know you called to remind me about your fitting today. But, I didn't forget."

"Actually Brandy," Sukenya laughed. "I called to give you the name and location of the designer who is making my bridal gown. It's Campbell's boutique right off of Madison."

"Oh," Brandy nonchalantly answered.

"Brandy," Sukenya pleaded in a whining voice. "Girl please don't be late. Because I really need your opinion and expertise today. Nicole says she can't make it because she is preparing for her court case and Alex says she has an appointment this afternoon that she cannot postpone, so you can't let me down Bran. You just can't."

"Oh please, Sukenya." Brandy laughed, "Stop whining. You know I'll be there. And as far as me being late, girl don't even go there. Because you and I both know although I have four babies to take care of, I'll get there long before you!" Again, the women laughed as they ended their call.

"I'll see you this afternoon at twelve," Brandy promised.

"Thanks Bran," an over excited Sukenya replied. "You're the best!"

As Sukenya hung up the phone, she smiled with a warm and secure feeling as she thought about Brandy. Sukenya thought about how they'd first met and laughed as she glanced over at an old picture of the two of them that she had hanging on her family room wall. She walked over stared at the picture and chuckled out loud as she said, "Who would have ever imagined that two silly freshmen trying out for their college band would have become such life long friends?"

Sukenya leaned over and touched the picture as she thought about those days and suddenly began to recite her old poem of yesteryear.

> *"Friends come a dime a dozen,*
> *When you really need them,*
> *They're no-where to be found."*

Sukenya moved in a little closer to study Brandy's face as she smiled and whispered. "But,

True friends come once in a lifetime,
They're there before you need them,
Anticipating your every move,
Making sure you know,
Whatever happens,
I'll be there,
Not just today when a crowd is around.
But tomorrow.
When it is Quiet..."

Sukenya had written and given the poem to Brandy on their graduation day from Norfolk State University, some twenty years ago. Twenty years later, they were still the very best of friends.

Friends who today, were planning a wedding that represented a dream that those young ladies, now women, had dreamed about oh so many years ago. The dream, that is, of finding and marrying their true prince charming and soul mate.

Brandy, however, had met her prince charming, Darius, during their senior year at NSU. He was, in all accounts, a good man. Darius was smart, funny and devoted to his wife and children. And although through the years, especially while trying to start a family, he and Brandy had gone through their tough moments, their love, trust and respect for one another never wavered. They were in every way soul mates.

"And now," Sukenya laughed. "Here we are preparing for my wedding, preparing for me to marry my prince charming." "*But?*" she asked herself. "*Is he my soul mate? Is he even my true prince charming?*" "Or," she sighed and said out loud, "am I simply settling for second best?"

These questions were never far from Sukenya's thoughts as she sat on the sofa in her family room and remembered her initial meeting with her fiancé Greg.

Three

Sukenya had met her fiancé Greg two years ago during a news conference convention in Washington DC. As one of the guest speakers at the convention, Sukenya had been asked to meet with the publicist overseeing the convention for a quick briefing on her speech she was to deliver. As the two business colleagues met, like most first meetings, they shook hands. Sukenya noticed how strong and secure his handshake was followed by a strange warm sensation she felt when he gently placed his left hand on top of her right hand. "*Humm,*" she thought to herself. "*No wedding band.*"

As she looked into his eyes, Sukenya noticed a calmness there that caused her heart to flutter. Along with a smile that seemed so sincere. And when he said, "Hello Sukenya, so nice to meet you." The sound of his voice made her feel oh so proud to be an African American woman. For standing less than two feet across from her was a tall, well-groomed, articulate and self-assured African American Man.

Who, she laughed, *later claimed to have known instantly that she was going to be the woman that he would one day marry*. For according to Greg, she was in his opinion, at five foot four with an hourglass figure and a look of mystery, simply amazing. An amazing woman with a poised and very princess like character that reminded him of someone of royalty. Possibly an African Queen.

Sukenya however, was not in anyway interested in anything other than a business relationship with Greg. She'd been hurt years ago, and vowed to focus all of her attention on her career and leave the men to themselves.

Therefore in the beginning Sukenya politely declined all of Greg's invitations.

"Dinner?"

"No thank you."

"Lunch?"

"Sorry I'm busy today."

"A snack?"

"I'm not hungry."

"How about a glass of water?" Greg once asked.

But Sukenya would only give Greg the same polite answer. "No thank you Greg. But, thank you for asking." Sukenya felt she had her reasons for declining Greg's invitations, but also knew they had nothing to do with Greg who on the other hand was quite persistent.

Not to the point of being a nuisance, she laughed. *But simply because he was so nice and so polite.*

Greg would send flowers, balloons, emails and cards. But like many times before, Greg's pleas and invitations always fell on deaf ears.

Greg however, didn't care, especially when the other guys would tease him for trying so hard. Because in his heart, Greg knew, "there was something different about Sukenya."

It was, he once told her, "The way she walked, the way she spoke, and the way she laughed." But most of all, Greg admired the way Sukenya embraced others, warm and sincere. And would often say, "she is such a natural beauty, with a distant sadness in her eyes, a sadness that shows, even when she laughs."

In Greg's opinion Sukenya was a rare jewel. A jewel that craved love, but was too afraid to let anyone in. And yet, he was determined to have Sukenya. No matter how long it took, he was going to make it happen. Because bottom line, Greg was in love with Sukenya, and everything about her.

"God," he would often say. "If only she would give me a chance. I would do everything in my power to remove the sadness from her eyes and turn it into joy."

Then one evening during an awards dinner for the Media at Chelsea Piers in New York, Sukenya received an award on a news segment she had created on being single in the new millennium.

Greg, who was covering the entire show; walked up to Sukenya and said as he handed her a glass of champagne, "Congratulations on your award Sukenya."

"Thanks Greg," Sukenya replied as she sipped on her glass of champagne. "It's great to be recognized by your peers."

"Sukenya, you are recognized by more than just your peers, because I recognized you and your talents a long time ago. What I don't understand," he laughed, "is, what's wrong wit em!" *Referring to other men*, "because, girl, you are so fine, I'd drink your bath water if you asked me to, with you in it!"

At first, Sukenya looked up at Greg, with a look of utter surprise and skepticism. But then, she began to smile. Sukenya smiled and smiled until finally she burst into a wild laugh. Spewing champagne all over Greg's tailor made suit.

"Oh my God," an embarrassed Sukenya shrieked. "I'm so sorry Greg for watering down your suit, but I couldn't help myself," she laughed as she tried to wipe off his suit, "because that was such a played out remark."

As Sukenya looked up at Greg, she let out a hysterical howl, and said, "Greg if only you could see your face. Your face looks like you're saying, 'oh god, please tell me I did not just say what I was thinking out loud!!'"

"Ha. Ha. Ha," a somewhat embarrassed Greg replied. "It's great to see that you're a mind reader too Sukenya."

Sukenya laughed because of Greg's played out statement followed by the look of utter disbelief and embarrassment on his face. It was during that particular evening that Sukenya agreed to go out on a non-business related date with Greg.

After a year of praying and trying, Greg had finally been given his chance. With that chance, Greg showered Sukenya with the little things, like in-depth conversations. Conversations that sometimes lasted for days. Days that sometimes included long wonderful weekend getaways where, they would walk and talk on moonlit beaches or listen to the ocean while sitting on the balcony of an ocean cruise liner.

"Sukenya," Greg would often say, "as long as you have something to say I will listen. No matter what time of the day or night, my ears are yours. If your day is full of stress, and you want to vent, I'll be an unbiased listener. If your shoulders feel heavy and you need a hand, take mine, for I give it to you freely. Just trust and know that all that I do Sukenya is done out of my sincere desire to make you happy."

For this reason, Sukenya allowed Greg to breathe life and love into her heart and soul. He had broken the cold lock and chain from around her heart and replaced it with warmth and love. Six month's later, the two were engaged to be married. And although Sukenya seemed happy, the sadness in her eyes remained.

Four

Sukenya heard the clock strike twelve and woke up out of her daze. "Oh shoot," she said as she quickly jumped up off of the sofa, grabbed her jacket and keys and ran out of the house. "I'm going to be late for my own fitting. Once again, Brandy's right," she laughed as she started her car. "Because she's going to get to Paul's long before I do."

Sukenya sped across town, pulled into the parking lot, parked her car and quickly walked up to Paul, laughing and waving her hands saying, "I know, I know," while Brandy stood near the fitting room inside of Campbell's boutique with her hands on her hips, tapping her feet, smiling and looking at her watch.

"Brandy please don't be late," she laughed as she followed Sukenya into the fitting room.

"That's right, Brandy," Sukenya's designer Paul teased. "Sukenya is forty-five minutes late. Isn't she? Suk doll, I sure hope you don't do this on your wedding day."

Ten minutes later...

"Oh, Sukenya!" Brandy cried out, as she placed her hands up to her mouth.

"Do you really like It Brandy?" Sukenya asked. "Yes, Girl, your gown is absolutely beautiful, Sukenya, it is you all over!"

Sukenya had worked with the finest designer on this side of the east coast, by way of Kenya. The wedding gown she'd sketched in her eighth grade home economics class was no longer her dream gown, but now a creation of her own. Having hand-picked every detail, Sukenya's gown had been made out of the finest African fabrics.

The top was a sleeveless form fitting corset design with white oyster pearls hand sewn throughout the entire front and back. The full bottom was bell shaped with oyster beads sewn in the design of little crosses outlined in platinum dyed pearls and white organza scallops.

Her twelve foot train was made out of pure Egyptian silk with the same oyster beads and platinum pearls set in an embroidered cross down the middle of the train with the initials SH for Sukenya Hollingsworth and GH for Greg Hollingsworth on each side of the cross.

As Brandy marveled at Sukenya standing there in her wedding gown, looking absolutely beautiful, she became overwhelmed with emotion. She was so ecstatic about her oldest and dearest friend finally getting married that she lost it. "Oh Sukenya," she cried. "You are truly going to be the most beautiful bride in New Jersey. After all of this time Suk, *This* is the wedding you so deserve. Along with *all* of the happiness in the world, and then some."

"Brandy," Sukenya chuckled as she handed her a Kleenex. "Stop your blubbering. Girl you are so dramatic. I told you along time ago. God knows and does all things for a reason. We may not understand it then, but when the time is right, all is revealed. So dry your tears, and help me get out of this dress," Sukenya laughed.

As Brandy helped her friend out of her gown, she smiled as she remembered a poem Sukenya had given her some twenty years earlier.

Friends come a dime a dozen,
When you really need them,
They're no-where to be found.
True Friends come once in a lifetime...

Five

"I will be glad when this damn case is over!" Nicole shouted, as she raced to the courtroom although she was in her car alone. "I am sick of this. And I don't know how much longer I can take it. Why, Why Lord, must I go through this? What is the purpose? I hate them. I hate them. I hate them!" she screamed. "Oh Lord, please forgive me. I don't hate them. I can't hate them. I will not allow them to make me hate!"

Nicole pulled her car over and began to sob. "I just want this to be over," she cried.

"I just want this to be over. I need this to be over. I really need for this to be over. So I can get on with my life. My life... My life..."

"My life?" she sarcastically asked herself while shaking her head back and fourth. "What life?" she moaned as the memories and the pain of her past came rushing back like a tidal wave.

It had been four years since Nicole's admittance to Saint Mary's Psychiatric Facilities.

"She needs rest." Nicole remembered the doctor saying to a relative.

"How long will she have to stay?"

"I'm not sure," the doctor replied in a somber but firm voice. "You see. Nicole is suffering from severe depression, and after her accidental overdose. (It had been no accident.) It would be best if she remained here for a while..."

Six

Nicole had always been on top of her game. After graduating summa-cum-laude with a dual degree in Computer Science and Economics, Nicole thought the world was hers. Prior to her graduation, she had accepted a lucrative position at one of the top computer firms in the country.

The company known as Triscope Corporations was considered to be a very diversified company who upheld their equal employment opportunity rules with pride and joy. Their zero tolerance for any form of discrimination was often mentioned in numerous business articles.

"Here, in this company, everyone regardless of their race, religion, color and or sexuality is considered equal," Triscope's owner and CEO, Mr.

Fred Hines was often quoted as saying. "In order for our company to operate and win in this business, we must all work together. We must all work with respect, honor and dignity for one another because at Triscope, we are all leaders. We are all owners. And here at Triscope is where diversity begins."

Therefore, in the beginning, Nicole's career at the company seemed perfect. She was smart and aggressive. She didn't mind working. As a matter of fact, she absolutely loved it. For in her opinion, Triscope was truly a fun place to work.

As time went on, her ideas and computer savvy earned her numerous awards within the company. Not to mention, she was making Triscope an enormous amount of money. Here, at Triscope, is also where Nicole met her husband Brian.

In only three short years, the recent newlywed had made an impressive name for herself. So it was no surprise to anyone when at the mere age of twenty-five, Nicole was named Director of Wireless Systems. According to Nicole, "Everything in my life is perfect." She had a job she loved and a new husband she adored. But a year after her testimony, all was about to change.

***

8:00 am

"Good morning Ashley," a well-rested and tanned Nicole said as she walked into her office.

"Good morning Nicole," her assistant answered in a strange voice.

"Ashley?" she asked. "Is everything all right?" Instead of replying, Ashley burst into tears.

"Ashley, what's wrong?"

"It's Fred," she cried. "We tried to call you last night, but your housekeeper said you and Brian were still in Jamaica on vacation."

"Yes that's right," Nicole answered. "We took the first flight out this morning. Brian and I came here straight from the airport. But you mentioned Fred, Ashley. What about Fred?"

"Nicole, there was a horrible plane crash, and Fred was on it."

"A Plane Crash!" Nicole screamed. "When?"

"Late last night," Ashley answered while blowing her nose.

"How?" Nicole asked.

"We're not sure. One minute the plane was flying and then it just blew. Nicole, the plane just blew up in mid air. It disintegrated over the ocean," Ashley quietly said with sorrow. "There was nothing or no one left."

44

As the news of her now deceased boss registered, Nicole slowly lowered herself into her chair and began to cry. "Oh my God!" she cried. "Oh my God! Not Fred, not Fred, not my sweet Fred."

She repeated the words over and over, shaking her head back and forth trying to absorb the devastating news as she remembered him laughing and saying, *"Nicole, you're married now. Go to Jamaica with your husband and have some fun. I'll handle the symposium and fill you in when you return from your vacation."*

Suddenly, Nicole gasped as she looked up in horror and placed her hands over her mouth. She remembered her last conversation with Fred and realized that *she too* was supposed to have been on the now doomed flight.

Nicole placed her face inside the cup of her hands, and began to weep, to bellow, to cry out. "Poor Fred," she mumbled between sobs. "Poor, poor Fred." "How" the totally devastated Nicole asked herself over and over between sobs, "could this have happened to such a wonderful and humble man?" Nicole leaned back in her chair with her eyes closed as her tears flowed freely from their corners, rapidly moving down the sides of her cheeks and meeting at her chin dripping like water from a broken faucet down the center of her white silk blouse, as she somberly remembered Fred.

Fred had been the CEO of Triscope Corporation for over thirty years. He had started the company at the young age of twenty-two and now in prime of his life at the mere age of fifty-two, he was dead. It was he who had started the open door policy at Triscope and made it into a family oriented company.

"This is not my company," he would often say. "It is our company. Where, in order to make this company successful we all have a part to play. We are therefore all equal, from the custodians, to the cooks, to the CEO. Here we all share the role as owners of Triscope. Where we support one another as a family."

Fred made sure any and everyone who worked for Triscope felt and believed in his theory.

As Nicole remembered those wonderful words of Fred's, she rocked her body back and forth in her chair while slowly moving her head from side to side and sobbed openly as she said,

"Good-bye, Fred. Good-bye. And Thank You. Thank you for giving me the opportunity to learn and to grow to understand and to know. We will all miss you Fred. I, my friend and mentor, will miss you. Good-bye Fred," she somberly sobbed. "Good-bye."

Seven

It took six months before a new CEO was named. Triscope hired an outsider by the name of Mr. Tom Jackovich to prepare the company for The New Millennium.

"The year two thousand is only a stone's throw away," Mr. Jackovich would often say. "We, therefore, must be ready for Y2K."

As with most new management comes new ideas, and change. Mr. Jackovich's idea of change was, "*Let me bring in my own people.*" At first the changes were subtle. Christmas parties were the first to go and the company picnics were by invitation only. The number of custodians were cut in half and given more tasks, while the administrative assistants were reassigned to an archaic secretarial pool and Nicole's assistant was suddenly let go.

Life at Triscope was no longer about family, and the company's rumor mill was running over with stories about Triscope's new CEO. For on more than one occasion, Mr. Jackovich was said to have been overheard saying, "Start giving women special titles, next they will try and start running their own companies. There are only a few places a woman belongs, and my boardroom is not one of them!"

One day after a grueling meeting with Tom, Nicole asked herself, "How could the board have hired such a male chauvinist? And why? Especially in this age and time. How, in our world of cellular phones, world-wide web and space dominance, are there men who still believe that a woman's place is not in the board room? How could Triscope's board of directors have hired such a man who believes we, as women are only good enough for one room? Well maybe two." She laughed as she said, "The kitchen and the bedroom...the kitchen and the bedroom."

Nicole however was smart. She'd been with the company long enough to know how to work around Tom. Or so she thought.

As time went on, three years to be exact, Nicole's opinion of the company continued to decline. Triscope was no longer a fun place to work. It was no longer "Our Company." We were now simply "employees of Triscope. What a joke," Nicole sighed, as she sat in her office and reached for her ringing phone.

"Nicole, hi this is Sheila, Tom's secretary. I'm calling to inform you that Mr. Jackovich has rescheduled the contract-signing meeting with the CEO of Sintech from 10:00 this morning to 2:00 this afternoon."

"Two o'clock?" Nicole asked. "Why so late? According to the message I received earlier, the CEO of Sintech arrived last night."

"Look Nicole," Sheila snapped. "I don't know why the meeting was rescheduled. I was just told to relay the message to you. If you have any questions, I would suggest that you speak directly with Mr. Jackovich. Who, at the moment, is unavailable."

"Excuse Me?" a somewhat surprised Nicole asked and replied in an agitated voice, "Sheila, please don't take that tone with me! I asked you a simple question concerning a very important meeting. And Sheila, for the record, IT is my JOB to probe and ask questions. Especially when it has to do with a billion dollar contract!" Nicole took a deep breath and said, "Now, if you cannot answer my questions or do not know the answers then please, just say so. But don't you ever speak to me in that tone again! Do I make myself clear?"

"Crystal," Sheila answered in a low but perturbed voice. "Would you like for me to ask Tom to call you?" she asked, in a very professional tone.

"Yes," Nicole answered. "Please have him call me ASAP. Thank You Sheila." As Nicole hung up the phone, she remembered the day Tom hired Sheila, which made her laugh. *"It definitely was not for her brains,"* she thought.

Nicole waved her hand as if to dismiss her thoughts and mumbled under her breath, "That's Tom's problem. I have more important things to worry about. Such as, why, would he suddenly cancel this morning's meeting? *I know Tom and I were here until midnight with the contract attorneys signing our portion of the checks and contracts,"* she silently thought. *"And I also know in order to be here today to sign his portion of the contracts and to finalize the deal, Mr. Sanjay of Sintech, arrived in the United States late last night."*

"Humph," Nicole said as she asked herself out loud, "I wonder if Tom is sick?"

Nicole then leaned back in her plush leather chair and looked around her very posh corner office, surrounded by windows and overlooking a beautiful lake. She scanned the room with her eyes and remembered how excited she'd been when she was promoted to Director of Wireless Systems. She also remembered how happy she was and how proud everyone was of her.

"*Congratulations on your promotion Nicole, you deserve it!*" was the normal tune for almost a month after her promotion. Back then, everyone was happy for her, from the cooks to the CEO.

For several weeks after her promotion, her office was filled with well wishes and flowers from all over the country, including competitive outside firms.

She'd even posed in a photo layout with Essence *Magazine* for an upcoming issue on *Young and Powerful Black Women in Business.*

"Yes," Nicole said out loud. "Those were some of the happiest moments in my life. But, that was five years ago...When Fred was alive. Now," she sighed. "All I do is work here."

Nicole stood up, walked over to her window and stared outside. Where she observed two geese playing in the lake. *"Humph,"* she thought. *"If only life were that simple."* Nicole continued observing the geese and began to daydream...

"This merger between Triscope and Sintech is going to be one of the largest mergers ever. By acquiring Sintech, we are going to have close to 300,000 employees world wide, with enough revenue

51

and stock options to bring in an astonishing amount of business."

"Hell," she chuckled, "I may just be able to retire at the mere age of thirty-five." Nicole laughed at the thought, as she remembered her initial meeting with the CEO of Sintech.

She had flown half way around the world, met with and won the merger from a company who had very little experience in conducting business with women and zero experience with a Black woman. This concept was so foreign that during Nicole's initial meeting, she was sent a woman escort to accompany her to a special welcoming party for the 100 guests also bidding for Sintech's contract. However when she arrived at the reception dinner, to Nicole's amazement, she was the only actual businesswoman there. And, even more peculiar were the other 99 businessmen who were also accompanied by similar women escorts all dressed in the same sensuous black dress as Nicole's escort!

By the time the CEO of Sintech realized the very eccentric and embarrassing situation, he apologized profusely to Nicole. Nicole however, being the confident Black woman that she was, had accessed the situation early on. She therefore, responded with the grace and wit that had gotten her out of many sticky situations in the past, by simply smiling and saying, "Nonsense, Mr. Sanjay. Sir. My escort and I are in very good company and if I must say... I absolutely love the black dress effect. Besides, in my country, I've learned to adapt to situations that were far beyond this innocent faux pas. I, Mr. Sanjay, am a guest in your country."

Nicole paused for a moment and then said, "There is an old saying that we say back home in the United States. 'When in Rome, do as the Romans do.' Well, Mr. Sanjay, tonight I'm in Rome by way of the Middle East. Although," she chuckled with confidence, "I thought it was strange that my name card said Nick on it and not Nicole. But now I see and understand why," she laughed. The entire room began to laugh as well.

Because of Nicole's honest response, she won the account hands down. Mr. Sanjay was so impressed with Nicole's dark complexion, beauty and wit, he agreed to fly to the United States and close the merger himself.

"Which," Nicole said out loud, "is going to occur in about 15 minutes."

It was now a quarter to two. As Nicole prepared for the meeting, she realized Tom had never returned any of her phone calls. Nicole enjoyed her job; but she simply hated how Tom treated her. Little did she know, her problems were just beginning.

As Nicole walked into the conference room she had a funny sick feeling in the pit of her stomach. *Nerves,* she thought as she brushed off the feelings. Nicole was the first to arrive. So she thought.

As Nicole looked around the room, she noticed the room was not properly set up for a meeting. The feeling in her stomach returned as she reached for the phone located in the center of the large oak conference table and called Tom's secretary.

"Sheila, hi, this is Nicole. I'm in the conference room, but no one is here. Did Tom change the conference room when he rescheduled the meeting from this morning?"

"Conference room?" a puzzled Sheila asked.

"Yes," Nicole answered. "Remember you called me this morning and stated that Tom had rescheduled our meeting for this afternoon?"

There was a dead silence on the other end of the receiver.

"Hello, Sheila are you there?" Nicole asked.

Finally Sheila answered. "I never called you," she slowly replied. "Although. I thought it seemed a little strange that you decided not to attend one of the most important meetings in Triscope's history."

"WHAT!" Nicole screamed. "Sheila, you called me at 7:30 this morning, don't you remember?" she asked.

"I'm sorry Nicole." Sheila laughed. "But I couldn't have called you, because I was at my 7:30 dentist appointment this morning. Nothing serious, just a regular clean."

"Look Sheila!" Nicole quickly interrupted. "Don't play games with me! Because I know you called me this morning, so cut the crap."

Again Sheila laughed and said, "Sorry Nicole, but you really need to slow down. Because, I think you're starting to hallucinate. Tom and Mr. Sanjay waited patiently for you until around 11:00. Finally after your big no-show, they decided to complete the final phase of the merger without you."

"WHAT!!!" Nicole screamed as she slapped the front of her forehead.

"However," Sheila continued, totally ignoring Nicole's outburst. "It is a good thing your junior director was there to cover for you."

"Junior director?" A surprised Nicole asked. "What junior direct? You know what Sheila, just, forget, it!" Nicole snapped, as she quickly asked, "Where is Tom now?"

"Oh." Sheila laughed, "He's in his office. Would you like for me to..." BAM!

IN THE NAME OF SISTERHOOD

Nicole slammed the phone down in Sheila's ear and quickly walked towards Tom's office.

As Nicole entered Tom's office, there stood Mr. Sanjay with his coat tossed over his left arm and shaking Tom's hand with his right hand.

When Mr. Sanjay and Nicole's eyes met, he smiled and said, "Nicole how wonderful it is to see you again. I'm sorry you weren't able to meet with us this morning. I had looked so forward to seeing you again. After all," he continued, "it was because of your grace and wisdom that Triscope won our contract."

Mr. Sanjay then walked over, took Nicole's hand, turned to Mr. Jackovich, and said,

"You should be very proud of this young woman. She will one day make an impressive name for herself as well as this company."

Tom interrupted Mr. Sanjay by saying, "Yes. Nicole is a very impressive *person*. That's why," now looking directly into Nicole's eyes. "I can't imagine what could have been so important that you would blow off our meeting this morning Nicole. Where were you?" he asked. Tom chose his words very carefully. He wanted to make Nicole look bad, but not at the expense of offending the very wealthy Sheik in the process.

At first, Nicole stared deep into Tom's eyes with a look as cold as Ice. "*Where was I?*" She thought to herself. "*What kind of fucking game is he playing? This Bastard sabotages my entire operation and is now trying to make me look like an idiot!*" Nicole however, being the professional that she was, simply smiled and answered, "Tom, you know I would never blow off a meeting. Besides, while this may be the biggest merger ever in the history of Triscope. My objective was to acquire the contract. Mr. Sanjay is here, and from the looks of things, has signed Sintech over to Triscope. So as far as I am concerned Tom, my job was done."

"And," interrupted Mr. Sanjay. "Tom If I may interrupt," he firmly said. "Nicole's job was performed, quite well. The mere fact that I flew here in person to sign the contract is a testimony in itself of Nicole's superb accomplishment!" Mr. Sanjay was now fully aware of what was going on as he turned and winked at Nicole.

Tom, unaware of Mr. Sanjay's gesture, continued his assassination of Nicole's character by waving his hand and saying, "Oh it really doesn't matter where you were Nicole. I just thought after all of the hard work you put into acquiring Sintech, it's a pity you missed witnessing the actual signing of the most lucrative contract in Triscope's history. It was however a very smart move on your part, to send in your new junior director to represent you."

Just as Tom completed his sentence in walked the new junior director, Mr. Robert Fauken. Robert was 6ft-4in with blond hair and these amazing blue eyes and had a smile that could knock your socks off. However, he looked all of twenty-one. Robert a recent college graduate from Tom's alma mater was just happy to be there. As he began to speak, Nicole knew instantly, he was no match for her.

Robert extended his hand and said, "Nicole, I'm so happy to finally meet you."

"*Idiot!*" she quietly thought, but was very satisfied, because Tom's plan had backfired, "*thanks to my new junior director,*" she silently chuckled as she said, "Why Robert, what do you mean happy to meet me? I'm the one who sent you here to represent me today. Isn't that right Tom?" Nicole asked as she turned and stared deep into his eyes.

Mr. Sanjay, now quite amused by the entire scene, promptly cleared his throat and said, "Nicole, it has been an honor and a pleasure doing business with you. I know our paths will cross again one day." Sanjay frowned as he turned to look at Tom and said in a dry voice, "Tom this is my first trip to America, which I've always been told, is the land of great opportunities and the home of the free. I bid you all a good day," and abruptly left.

Nicole also left Tom's office without uttering a single word. This was the third time Tom had tried to undermine her and she was livid. Nicole knew she could not go off on Tom the way she wanted to. "After all... He Is the CEO," she muttered as she stormed into her office and slammed herself into the seat of her plush leather chair. *I mean I've heard of the glass ceiling, but this is crazy.* "Tom is making my ceiling cement." she huffed out loud. Nicole knew something had to be done, but what?

For the past two years, Tom had tried to undermine Nicole's work. He wanted her out! But he knew, because of her track record and length of time at Triscope it would not be an easy task. On several occasions, Tom set Nicole up for failure and each time, she came out on top.

He had purposely sent Nicole overseas to the Middle East to work on the Sintech deal. Simply because he knew it was a male-dominated country. To his amazement, not only did she win the contract, she set the merger up to be the most lucrative deal in the history of Triscope. So, instead of being elated, the contract only made Tom angrier and more determined to get Nicole out.

At an invitation-only banquet to celebrate the success of the merger, Tom's only comment to Nicole was, "Now that the deal is closed, why don't you go home Nicole, make some babies and leave this kind of work to the men?"

"Excuse me Tom," Nicole snapped. "Besides your comment being way out of line, my husband and I are happy just the way we are."

To be honest, Nicole's long and crazy hours were starting to take a toll on her marriage. She was working all hours of the day. Including the wee hours of the morning. Sometimes returning home from work between two and three o'clock in the morning at least two out of seven days a week.

"Nicole!" Brian would often say. "You are married to me! Not Triscope!"

Nicole knew Brian was right, but she wouldn't quit or just simply could not quit. She refused to allow Tom to break her. "After all," she once told Brian. "I was here long before Tom. Why do I have to leave simply because some bigot wants me out? Besides Brian," she pleaded. "Fred worked too hard to make this company what it is today."

As months passed, Tom became more and more ruthless. He named Nicole and Robert co-directors of Triscope International Systems. And within one year, promoted Robert as senior director over Nicole. To add insult to injury, Nicole was asked to make the formal announcement at the officers' banquet!

"*This,*" she silently hissed as she walked off of the podium, "*is the final straw.*" Nicole reported Tom to the company's local human resources department. However, to her surprise, Nicole was reprimanded for not being a team player.

"A team player?" a shocked Nicole replied. "This is my career we're talking about!"

Nicole's argument fell on deaf ears. Especially since unbeknownst to her, the head of personnel had been hand picked by Tom and was very loyal to his boss.

Nicole then took her complaint to the director of human resources, where she supplied the director with numerous documents, dates and cancelled plane tickets to validate her complaint. Once again she was told, "I'm sorry Nicole, but there is nothing I can do." According to the Director, "Tom could not be touched."

"I don't understand it," a bewildered Nicole said aloud as she walked out of the director's office. "It is as if someone higher up is responsible for Tom's behavior."

Eight

Tom's very ruthless behavior began to take its toll on Nicole. She began suffering with excruciating headaches, bouts of insomnia, and horrible stomach cramps.

"Nicole, you're stressed and need to relax," her doctors warned.

"Relax?" she asked. "How can I relax when I have a pool of sharks surrounding me just waiting for the right moment to strike?"

Although Nicole knew her doctors were right, she refused to listen. While at work, Nicole tried to act as if she was still on top of her game. Inside however, she was slipping deeper and deeper into a state of depression. Nicole would drive to a park on the other side of town where no one knew her and sit and stare out at the trees, the lake and the wild life.

There, she would gather her thoughts, talk to her God and cry.

"Why Lord," she would say, "is this happening to me? What have I done? How is it that this one individual can cause such hardship and misery in my life? I don't understand it. I've tried and I've tried to reason with him and to show him that I am all for Triscope succeeding. But for some reason Lord, it is not good enough. No, I guess he thinks I'm not good enough. I know that this is just a job, but it is a job in which I love. Not just the job in itself, but the people who work there as well. For they too knew and understood all that Fred stood for when he was alive. That is, the trust, the respect and the camaraderie that we had for one another. Can one man truly take all of that away? Help me to see Lord the reasoning behind this. Because Sir, to put it bluntly he is slowly stealing my joy from within."

Nicole would then drive back across town where her life seemed perfect.

After twelve years at Triscope, Nicole's career was spiraling out of control and Tom was enjoying every moment of it. However, during the past three months Tom had become very quiet, almost too quiet. Nicole mistakenly took this as a sign of, "The storm finally being over." When in fact, it was just the opposite, because for Nicole, the eye of the storm was just beginning.

On June 12th at 8:00am, exactly twelve years and six months after Nicole walked into Triscope as an intern from Norfolk State University, she was called into the director of human resources' office for what she thought was a follow up to her complaint against Tom. Once there, to Nicole's surprise, there sat Tom.

At first she thought, "Finally!" But then noticed two other men both dressed in dark blue suits sitting in the office as well. Now clearly confused, Nicole asked the director of human resources, "What's going on Mr. Klein?"

"Nicole," he said at first in a whisper but then clearer as he handed her a red folder. "There seems to be a problem. I've recently come across some information that I think you need to explain."

As Nicole took the folder, her hands trembled, although she didn't understand why.

Nicole opened the folder, and observed several cancelled checks. Each check had been made out to various individuals for a substantial amount of money. And while the names on the checks did not look familiar, the signature at the bottom of the checks did. They were Nicole's!

Once Tom noticed the surprised look in Nicole's eyes, he began his final reign by saying, "Nicole, Can you explain this?"

"Explain what?" Nicole asked.

"Explain how and why the cancelled checks you're observing are made out to individuals we do not know," he snapped.

"How should I know?" she replied, while waving the cancelled checks in the air. "I've never seen any of these names before, and I sure as hell didn't sign any of these!" But to Nicole's amazement the signature on the bottom of the cancelled checks were clearly hers.

"Mrs. Carpenter," Are you saying that the signatures on these checks are not yours?" asked one of the unfamiliar men sitting in the office dressed in a dark blue suit.

"That's exactly what I'm saying," Nicole replied. "And who may I ask are you?"

The man in the dark suit stood up, walked over towards the door as if to block Nicole from leaving and replied by saying, "My name is Detective David Cross, I'm with the Federal Bureau of Investigations."

"The FBI!" Nicole shrieked in a high-pitched voice. "What the hell is going on!" she asked.

"What is going on, replied the second gentleman also dressed in blue, is a trail of cancelled checks worth over $300,000 dollars."

"And Mrs. Carpenter," interrupted Mr. Cross, "they all point to you."

"To me!" Nicole shouted.

"Yes," Tom grinned, "to you."

"Look," Nicole replied in an attempt to reason with the men, "I'm sure there's been some type of misunderstanding, because not only did I not sign any of these checks, I've never seen any of these names before in my life!"

"Life," mocked Detective Cross, "is exactly what you're looking at. Life for embezzling more than $300,000 dollars over a six-month period. You see Mrs. Carpenter, we've been following your trail of deceit for some time now. These checks," the detective abruptly waved the checks in Nicole's face, "were written out to potential customers and deposited into dummy accounts on their behalf by none other than you! The only problem is," he laughed, "they are all deceased! And," he shouted, "since you are this big time director who has been writing checks at the same bank for the past seven years, the bank never became suspicious. You would have gotten away with it had it not been for Sheila,

Tom's secretary discovering the cancelled checks in a pile of work set aside for the shredder!"

"What!" Nicole screamed in a piercing high-pitched tone as her voice began to quiver and her eyes filled up with tears. "I never signed any of these checks," she quickly denied as she looked at the checks one by one. Nicole's tears began to stream down her cheeks as she asked in a loud and dazed voice, "Why would I try and embezzle money from this company? I would never steal from Fred's company and," she hissed, "I'm not exactly poor! After all, I am in a triple six-figure salary range."

"Nicole!" interrupted Tom as he handed her another cancelled check. "Are you saying this is not your signature?"

Nicole observed the check and began to cry uncontrollably, because the signatures were definitely hers.

"Nicole!" Tom bellowed. "We're waiting for an answer!"

"I never signed these checks!" Nicole cried.

"So Mrs. Carpenter, are you saying that this is not your signature?" Detective Cross asked.

"Yes," Nicole answered. "It is my signature. But I never ..."

"Nicole Carpenter!" Detective Cross quickly interrupted in a cold and harsh tone. "We are placing you under arrest for the embezzlement of more than $300,000 dollars!"

"WHAT?" Nicole screamed, "I never signed any checks! I never deposited any checks! I'm innocent!" she screamed. "I'm innocent!" she screamed again.

The detectives abruptly placed Nicole's hands behind her back and began to place a set of handcuffs around her wrists. The sensation of the cold steel handcuffs tightening around her wrists made her body go limp, as if she were about to faint.

Tom, however, immediately embraced Nicole and held her up. But before he let her go, Tom leaned in ever so close to Nicole and calmly whispered into her ear.

"Nicole, you should have gone home and made babies like I told you to do months ago. Now," he quietly snickered, "the only thing you'll be making will be license plates with the rest of your people."

Nicole looked up at Tom's smirking face. First in horror, then in utter disbelief and then in total anger! "You bastard!" she screamed as she lunged towards him.

The detectives immediately restrained Nicole and led her out of the office as she screamed, "I'm innocent ... I'm Innocent!" Mr. Klein, the head of HR, lowered his head in embarrassment and regret.

The detectives led Nicole out of the 12th floor office and began walking her towards the elevator, which happened to be fifty feet away.

Nicole was amazed that there were people standing everywhere. Some with their hands over their mouths in shock, while others who had worked with Nicole during the past twelve years simply lowered their heads in total disbelief and disgust as tears openly streamed down their cheeks. After all, this was no ordinary employee. This was Nicole! The woman who had worked her way up through the ranks during a time when the company was considered a fun and family oriented place to work.

"How?" many asked and wondered, as they pointed and whispered. "How could this have happened to Fred's protégé?"

As Nicole walked towards the elevator doors, she held her head up and looked straight ahead, never exactly meeting anyone's eyes. Amazingly, as she stepped onto the elevator and watched the doors close, Nicole remembered the look of every face she had passed on the way to the elevator.

"*How Lord?*" she silently asked as the elevator began to descend. "*And why Lord is this happening to* me? *I don't understand!*" She prayed, "*Please God, please help me to understand! because this can not be happening to me!*"

Nicole repeated her words over and over again as if trying to wake herself from a horrible dream. Sadly for her, this was no dream. This was real, this was humiliating, and this was definitely happening!

The elevator went straight to the bottom of the parking deck where an unmarked squad car sat waiting to speed Nicole off to jail.

Nine

O nce Nicole arrived at Police Headquarters, her nightmare continued. She was fingerprinted and interrogated for another five hours. Finally, at 2:00 am, Nicole was allowed to make her one phone call. The call, her one and only phone call was to her husband Brian. "Oh please Brian," she prayed out loud, as the phone began to ring. "Please baby pick up. *Please pick.*" The ringing suddenly stopped and Nicole began to cry and speak at the same time. "Brian, Brian," she heard herself say. "There has been a..."

"Hi you've reached the Carpenters," the answering machine answered back, "please leave a message."

Instead of replying Nicole turned and looked at the correctional officer as she heard her phone go dead. Nicole slowly lowered her head as she realized her one and only phone call had been useless. She was then led to a holding cell.

"Oh my God!" she gasped as the stench of urine and vomit hit her nose. Nicole immediately placed both hands over her nose in an attempt not to inhale the odor but it was impossible. Once inside the cell, Nicole's eyes scanned the small room where she noticed a small cot with a urine-stained mattress on it and a filthy toilet bowl with a half used roll of toilet tissue hanging from the handle that looked as dirty as the toilet. She flinched as she heard the sound of the heavy metal doors closing behind her followed by the unbelievably loud clicking sound of the doors locking.

Nicole quickly turned and looked up at the guard with pleading eyes. But it was useless.

"Try and relax," the woman correctional officer replied in a tone that answered Nicole's questioning eyes.

As the guard walked away, she yelled over her shoulder, "You're scheduled to see the judge this morning at 7:00 am sharp. Good luck," she shouted as she left the holding area.

Nicole then turned around and once again observed the urine-stained mattress. Slowly she pulled off her suit jacket and strategically placed it on one corner of the mattress facing the wall. Nicole then gradually sat on the jacket in a calculated way to make sure her body never actually touched the mattress or the wall. Afterwards, she carefully pulled her knees up tightly into her chest and wrapped her arms around them as she sorrowfully lowered her head into her arms.

Not to sleep, but rather to think.

Nicole had no idea as to who signed those checks. But she was sure of one thing. Tom was behind the entire fiasco! *"But how am I going to prove it?"* she asked herself.

Suddenly the lights in the holding area went out, leaving Nicole in total darkness. Although Nicole could not see anything, she could clearly hear other people moving around in their cells. She heard one women crying and cursing loudly, as another women talked on her imaginary cell phone while loudly passing gas and laughing out loud.

Nicole sobbed in silence as she shook her head back and fourth while whispering, "This isn't happening to me Lord. It just isn't! It can't be! It just cannot be happening to meee!"

Unfortunately for Nicole it was indeed happening. Her stint in total darkness seemed like an eternity. For during the entire night she never allowed sleep to be an option.

At 7:00 am Nicole was led out of the holding cell, and brought before a Judge, who posted her bail at $2 million.

"Two million dollars!" Nicole screamed as she turned and looked at her attorney with wide eyes.

Nicole's attorney quickly placed his hand on top of Nicole's shoulder and said. "Your honor, my client has never had so much as a parking ticket. Why are you placing her bail at such an enormous amount?"

"Why?" the judge asked in a surprised voice. "Just think about it," he replied. "You have one of the top and only African American female directors at Triscope Corporation charged with embezzling over a quarter of a million dollars. And you're asking me why her bail is so high? Hell," he chuckled. "She's practically a celebrity. Besides, in order for her to be released, she only needs to post ten percent."

Nicole used her home as collateral for bail and was immediately released. It was now 8:00 am, exactly twenty-four hours since Nicole's nightmare began.

Ten

Nicole arrived home 24 hours after she'd left for work. And because she was still wearing the same clothes from the day before, all she wanted to do was to get home, take off those horrible clothes and take a long hot bath. Instead, as Nicole pulled up onto her circular driveway, to her surprise, there, camped out all over her beautifully manicured front lawn, were news reporters from every radio and television station within one hundred miles.

"I don't believe this shit!" she said out loud as she stepped out of her car. Nicole was immediately attacked by a swarm of reporters from all sides of her beautiful home.

"Nicole!" one reporter shouted. "Is it true?" he asked.

"No comment!" Nicole snapped as she tried to go thru her garage. Unfortunately, reporters had it blocked. Nicole then made a mad dash up the driveway towards her front door praying her live in house keeper was there to open it and rescue her from the mob that was hot on her trail. As she placed her hand on the doorknob and turned it, the door opened!

"Thank you Jesus!" Nicole shouted as she quickly ran into the house.

Nicole didn't see who had opened the door, she just knew it opened and she was in.

As the door closed behind her, she began to focus. There was luggage everywhere! She then heard a click from the doorknob, which at first startled her as she suddenly remembered seeing her front door opening. At that same moment Nicole froze with fear as she realized, she never saw who opened it! Nicole slowly turned around towards the sound of the door, and to her relief, there stood Brian. Her husband!

"B... B... Brian!" she stuttered as she ran towards him with her arms opened wide. "Oh Brian," she cried. "You will never believe."

Brian reached out for Nicole, as if to console her but instead tightly grabbed her wrists and angrily glared at his wife. The look in his eyes was not that of a consoling husband, but rather the look of an angry man who was fed up with his wife, her job and their marriage.

"Nicole, it is eight o'clock in the morning," he finally whispered between his teeth as he slowly pulled his wife towards him and said. "When I asked you to let Triscope go, you ignored me. When I asked if we could start our family, you ignored me. When I asked if we could see a marriage counselor, you ignored me. So now Nicole, my dear sweet wife, It's my time... It's my time to ignore you! It's over!" he yelled.

With every sentence Brian's voice grew louder and louder. It was as if he were releasing all of the anger he had held inside for the past 10 years.

"Oh, oh, OVER!" Nicole replied. "Brian what are you talking about? I asked you for time and now!" Nicole snapped. "Is not the time for you to be ultra-dramatic! Because Brian, I'm in real deep trouble and I really need your support."

"My support! Brian yelled. "Huh," he snarled. "Nicole, you've never needed me for anything! Not for my support. Not for my love. Not for anything! It's always been about you Nicole. You and only you! Never me! Never us! Just you..."

Nicole knew Brian was to some degree correct but now she felt was not the time to bring it up or to admit it.

"Brian," Nicole pleaded, "I'll try harder," attempting to diffuse his anger. "I promise."

"Save your promises!" Brian snarled as he picked up his luggage and walked out of the same door he had just let Nicole in.

Part of Nicole wanted to run after him, but deep down the other part of Nicole was saying, *"Good riddance. Brian has been a hindrance to me ever since our third year of marriage. And why one might ask? Primarily, because he had not moved up within Triscope as quickly as me."*

Nicole took a long deep breath, and slowly walked up the stairs leading towards her bedroom. As she entered her bedroom, Nicole quickly removed every stitch of her clothes and allowed them to drop freely to the floor. *I'll have Bajee my housekeeper take these things and donate them to charity.* She thought as she turned and stared down at her pile of clothes. *Because I know I'm never wearing any of them again.* Nicole then walked into her bathroom and began to run a hot bath in her oversized garden tub.

As she poured her favorite jasmine scented bath gel into the tub, Nicole lit several candles and stared deeply into their heated flickers. As she climbed into the tub, she hit the jet stream button and slowly sank into her heated cocoon, where she once again stared into the flicker of the candles. Motionlessly allowing them to put her into a trance as she remembered her issues concerning Brian and the issues centering around two individuals working together at Triscope, with one doing very well, and the other doing moderately well but wanting more.

In the beginning, Nicole and Brian's marriage seemed perfect. But on a professional level, it was Nicole's career that was on fire. Every decision she made seemed to turn into gold.

"And why not?" she jokingly asked Fred during one of their many private moments. "I'm happy and I'm in love."

With a combination like that, Nicole was on top of the world and within a span of three years started receiving promotion after promotion. Which is also around the time when unbeknownst to Nicole, Brian's smiles started turning into little frowns.

"Damn Nicole," he once said. "That's three promotions to my one. After a while I guess I'll have to start calling you the man of the house."

"Oh Brian don't be silly. You're the only man in our house baby. Besides, our careers are just that careers. It is what we do outside of work that counts. You're an excellent developer who can do anything that you put your mind to. Just work harder Brian at doing what you do best, and trust me baby, your time to shine will come."

But it never did. Instead, Brian began resenting Nicole's success and on the two-year anniversary of Fred's death, he quit Triscope. To make matters worse, Brian wanted Nicole to quit as well. Nicole refused, leaving Brian feeling threatened and disrespected.

"How can I be considered the man of my house Nicole, when in reality you my very successful wife are the actual breadwinner?"

"How?" Nicole asked. "Brian, what is there to consider? We are in this together, why can't you understand that? Besides, my salary has nothing to do with how much I love and respect you as a man." Nicole soon realized that no matter how many times she attempted to reassure him Brian did not and just would not ever understand her point of view. So, as a way to try and keep peace and to not further bruise her husband's ego, Nicole stopped telling Brian when she received salary increases and promotions.

"It's a shame," she once confided in Alexandria. "Here I am the top female Director at Triscope and I can't even celebrate my recent promotion with my husband."

Alexandria sarcastically replied, "Fuck him Nicole. Brian is just jealous of your success. Hell you're the one who studied hard in college and graduated summa-cum-laude from Norfolk State. Don't you remember?" she asked. "Besides why should you now hold yourself back just to satisfy his ego? This is your life Nicole and your career not his... So enjoy your moment. After all girl you deserve it."

"You may be right Alexandria, but let's face it, no matter how successful you are, at the end of the day everyone wants someone to come home to. Someone to say hey baby how was your day? Someone to snuggle up with and massage your shoulders, your feet, your body and help you forget about all the stresses of that day."

"That's true Nikki, but not at the expense of minimizing who you are. Not at the expense of making you feel less than a woman. Not at the expense of stealing your joy. You see Nicole I guess what I'm trying to say is... we as women must learn to create our own happiness and be proud of our own accomplishments in life. And girl if need be, just git-cho-self a dog, a warm blanket, a good book and some AA batteries. Trust me," Alexandria sarcastically laughed, "you'll feel sooo much better in the morning."

"Alex," Nikki laughed while shaking her head back and forth. "You are truly one of a kind, but I hear ya though and I love you for your wonderful and gallant choice of words."

The two women continued celebrating Nicole's recent promotion together by emptying several bottles of Moet.

Nicole smiled as she remembered the conversations from her past and thought about her current problems while emerging from her long hot bath. Because now at the worst time in Nicole's life, her marriage was over and she was facing criminal charges for a crime she did not commit. For the first time in Nicole's life she had hit rock bottom.

How on earth am I going to get out of this? Nicole later asked herself. *"How can Brian leave me now, when I need him more than ever? What is going to happen to me? Better yet, who signed my name to those checks?"*

These questions pounded in Nicole's head for months, as she waited for her trial to begin. In the mist of it all, Brian served Nicole with divorce papers and was suing her for alimony!

As time went on, exactly six months from the day of her initial arrest, Nicole became a recluse in her own home. She refused phone calls and visitors.

While her *"Sisters"* Sukenya, Alexandria and Brandy encouraged her to fight and to not give in. The women even took turns spending the night at Nicole's home, and reminiscing about their old college days. The days when things were oh so simple...

They laughed and talked about how Brandy and Nicole met while trying to dissect a pig in their freshman biology class and how Brandy cried because she said the dead pig would never be able to have babies.

"Brandy you were always worried about babies!" Nicole laughed as she remembered that particular day.

"Yeah," Brandy laughed. "Thank God you were on my team Nick, otherwise, I would have surely gotten an ' F ' out of that class!"

Brandy also brought her children over to play and to help keep Aunty Nicole's mind off of her charges.

Although Nicole was able to put on a remarkable front for everyone, day-by-day, she was slipping deeper and deeper into a horrible state of depression.

In all of her life, Nicole had never felt this kind of pain and despair. After all, she had always been on top of her game. A game that she feared would now have to be played out in prison.

One evening while everyone else slept, and her house was quiet, Nicole thought on these things, and decided to sleep her pain away.

"Why not?" she thought as she swallowed each pill one by one. *I'd rather face death than face prison. Especially since I know I'm innocent.* "God please forgive me," she cried as she drifted off into a peaceful sleep.

Eleven

"Nicole? … "Nicole? … "Nicole? …" A voice cried out, snapping Nicole out of her past and returning her to the present.

"Wha … What," a startled Nicole answered as she realized where she was, still sitting in her parked car with her car engine running and her windshield wipers going a hundred miles a minute, scraping the dry glass with a loud thump, thump, thump sound as she noticed the rain had apparently stopped sometime ago.

"Nicole!" her attorney Mr. Christopher Bellows shouted. "I've been looking all over for you. Court starts in less than ten minutes!"

"Ten minutes?" a somewhat dazed Nicole asked. "What happened?"

"What happened?" Chris answered in a startled and rather surprised voice. "Nicole let's talk about this later. Because court starts in less than eight minutes, let's just take my car and go," he calmly said, as he quickly helped Nicole out of her car and into his car and sped off to the courthouse.

Apparently, while Nicole was recovering at St. Mary's psychiatric facilities, Tom's secretary Sheila confessed to scanning Nicole's signature off of the contracts Nicole had signed during the merger between Sintech and Triscope. Sheila also confessed to how she then scanned Nicole's name onto several checks and deposited them into several fictitious accounts. Afterward, she'd dress up in clothes similar to Nicole's and withdraw the money from various ATM Machines...

It took Nicole six months of intense therapy and daily visits from Alexandria, Sukenya and Brandy before she was able to recover from her *'accidental'* overdose, and depressive state. Upon Nicole's release, not only was she stronger than ever, she was livid. Livid and determined to make Tom and Triscope pay for her very stressful and embarrassing ordeal!

"Sheila may have scanned those checks," she said as she spoke to Mr. Christopher Bellows, "but I know Tom was behind it all, and Triscope did nothing to stop his reign of terror."

For this reason, Nicole filed a multi-million dollar lawsuit against Tom and Triscope. Tom and Triscope out-and-out denied all of her charges, and subpoenaed witness after witness into the courtroom to corroborate their denial. One by one, the employees of Triscope marched into the courtroom and denounced Nicole's claims by affirming how Sheila and only Sheila had acted alone in her plot to destroy Nicole. And today, as Nicole sat in the courtroom, their testimonies *were* no different than before.

Nicole saw her case unraveling right before her eyes. But instead of blaming her former co-workers for lying, she actually felt sorry for them. She felt that, in order for them to sit in a courtroom, swear on a Bible and then lie, Tom must have them under an unbelievable amount of pressure. *"They are no longer the people Fred once groomed,"* she silently thought, as the day's court session ended.

Twelve

"Oh shit!" Alexandria snapped as she limped to the trunk of her car and pulled out a pair of sneakers. "I can't believe my shoe heel just broke. Damn, that's what I get for buying these cheap ass shoes," she growled as she slipped on her sneakers. "Oh man am I going to be late. Oh well," she laughed and said, "Sorry to keep you waiting hon, but momma has to stop at the Mall first for a new pair of shoes. Hey what can I say? My baby is coming home today. So I have to and am going to look extra good for my man. Who has been on the road for the past three weeks, and is only going to be in town for a few days."

Alexandria, tall, beautiful and usually the life of any party, *except,* when it came to her husband James. When James was in town, Alexandria was the perfect wife. She was so good the girls often teased and called her Miss Daisy's twin. As a matter of fact, when James was in town, an actual sighting of Alexandria was far and few.

James, an airline pilot for one of the major airlines, traveled constantly. So when he was home, Alexandria loved him with all her heart. That is...when, he was home and today, James was coming home...

"Of all days for James to come home, it would be today," Alexandria sighed as she rushed to the airport. "Today, when Nicole has to appear in court for another round of *'let's beat the crap out of Nicole with a bunch of lies.'* Lord please don't let her break down." Alexandria prayed out loud. "Their day will come Nikki," she said out loud as she arrived at the airport. "I promise you, their day will come!!"

Suddenly, Alexandria saw a silhouette of a figure who in her opinion was the finest man she'd ever seen. When their eyes met, she couldn't control herself. Alexandria jumped out of her Lexus and ran straight into his arms. The two embraced and kissed with such passion, they both nearly suffocated from lack of air. As the two stopped kissing and gazed into each other's eyes, Alexandria suddenly began apologizing to the figure.

"Oh God!" she said as she stepped back. "What am I doing? I'm so sorry sir please forgive me," she said, sounding half embarrassed but really quite amused. "It's just that when I saw you I couldn't control myself." She laughed nervously.

"Well, do you do this sort of thing often?" he asked.

"Only when my husband is away," she apprehensively answered.

"So you're married?"

"Yes. Yes I am," Alexandria stuttered. "I am happily married to the most wonderful man on the planet!"

"Then why did you just kiss me like that?" he asked.

Alexandria shrugged her shoulders and replied in a dry voice, "Don't know... I guess it was the uniform." The two then looked at each other, and burst into an amusing laugh.

"Girl, you have some serious issues." James laughed.

"Likewise," Alexandria replied.

The two walked arm and arm back to their car, which in all the excitement, Alexandria had inadvertently left running.

As they drove away in their car, Alexandria turned and looked at James as he stared out of the window. Alexandria truly loved James. She loved the way he looked at her, the way he smiled at her and the way she felt when he held her in his arms. She especially loved the way he made love to her. Fully, completely, and never ending.

Alexandria observed his very handsome features. Features that she oh so loved, like the smoothness of his creamy cocoa chocolate complexion and the thickness of his full and luscious lips. The look of his well tapered beard, the feel of his thick trimmed mustache, and the power of his chiseled chin. "*Yes indeedy!*" she thought to herself. "*This fine black specimen is in every way, my true love, my soul mate!*"

"Keep your eyes on the road Alex," James teased. "I would like to make it home in one piece," he laughed.

"My eyes are on the road," Alexandria replied in a chuckle. "Besides, just because it took me four times to pass my driving test doesn't mean I can't drive."

"Tell that to my insurance company!" James laughed, as he stared at his very beautiful wife.

When he looked at Alexandria, James only saw love. Her love. His love. Pure love. James was in love with Alexandria's very being.

As James observed Alexandria, his mind wandered to the time of their initial meeting some twelve years earlier...

Thirteen

James and Alexandria had met twelve years ago while vacationing in Cancun. At the time the two met, Alexandria was attempting to show Nicole and Brandy how to skydive by way of a ground demonstration. As James observed the three women, he noticed and admired Alexandria's quest for adventure. He could clearly tell by her actions she knew nothing about skydiving. He was so amused by the scene he challenged her to an actual jump.

"Sure! Piece of cake," she laughed as she turned and winked at the other two women who stared in disbelief.

"Alex!" Nicole whispered. "What are you doing?" Alexandria simply shushed Nicole with the wave of her hand and asked James.

"What time shall we meet?"

"How about 6:00?" James answered.

"Oh, I simply love dusk dives," Alexandria mocked.

"Dusk?" James asked in a puzzled tone. "Oh I'm sorry I should have made myself clearer. I meant to say 6:00 am."

"AM!" Alexandria shouted as she jerked her head back. "Hell, I don't get up until noon!"

By now, Nicole and Brandy were cracking up laughing.

"Alex, you are on your own," Nicole laughed as she and Brandy walked away.

"Yes Alex please let us know how your 6:00 AM jump goes," Brandy laughed.

"Nice meeting you James," the two women said as they turned and walked down the beach, holding their stomachs from laughing so hard.

"That's Alex for you," Nicole laughed, "always putting her foot in her big mouth!"

The two women were now howling with laughter as they walked down the beachfront of their very beautiful resort.

"Damn, I can't let this dweeb know I don't know the first thing about skydiving," Alexandria mumbled under her breath. "Shoot all I was trying to do was get the attention of the brother who I saw teaching the class earlier. Where did this one come from anyway?" she asked herself, now totally engulfed in her own thoughts and completely ignoring James.

"Then what about tomorrow night at 8:00 pm?" James asked totally interrupting Alexandria's one on one conversation with herself.

"Excuse me," Alexandria asked.

"Skydiving," James answered and then asked, "Would you like to go skydiving tomorrow night at 8:00? Because I know a great place where we can skydive at night."

Alexandria could tell by his tone that he wasn't going to let her out of this challenge.

"Eight o'clock it is," she reluctantly answered.

"Great!" James replied. "Meet me here at 8:00 sharp and be prepared for the jump of your life." He chuckled as he walked into the lobby of the resort.

Alexandria knew she had bitten off more than she could chew, but she refused to let him know it. "Besides," she thought, "What's the worst that can happen?"

James knew Alexandria didn't know the first thing about skydiving especially when she agreed to go skydiving at night! But it didn't matter. Alexandria intrigued James's interest and he wanted to know more about her.

At 8:05, Alexandria arrived wearing a red string halter-top and a white pair of well-pressed capris with a matching pair of red and white two and a half inch wedge sandals.

"I hope I'm not over dressed," she sheepishly said.

"Oh no," James replied, "your attire is perfect," he smiled. "Shall we go?"

"Sure!" Alexandria answered. "Lets get this skydiving date over with," she mumbled under her breath.

"Excuse Me? Did you say something Alexandria?" he asked.

"Huh, oh, uh I was simply saying how wonderful the night sky looks," she quickly replied.

As the two walked towards the small twin-engine plane, Alexandria was sure James could hear her heart pounding.

My heart is pounding so loud, she silently thought. *The natives are dancing to the beat.* Yet, on the outside, Alexandria walked towards the plane as if she were the queen of skydiving.

Unbeknownst to her, James was so amused by the entire scene; he bit the corner of his lower lip to keep from falling to the ground with laughter.

As James opened the door to the plane, Alexandria stopped short, turned around and looked him directly into his eyes and asked, "Aren't we supposed to put on our helmets and life jackets first?"

Well James was totally out done. However, he continued to play it cool.

"Oh no Alexandria," he answered. "We'll put on our *lifejackets* and helmets once we're airborne."

"Okaaay," she replied and stepped into the small twin-engine plane. "Where's the pilot?" she asked as she fastened her seatbelt.

"You're looking at him," James answered with a boyish grin.

"You!" Alexandria shrieked in a loud voice as her seatbelt buckle snapped into place.

"That's right," he answered as he started the planes twin engines. "I'm your pilot for tonight's jump."

"You!" Alexandria screamed again, as she felt the plane moving rapidly down the runway and quickly lifting off of the ground. "Oh shit," she screamed as she wrapped her arms around the straps of the seat belts and tightly folded her arms together under her breasts as her balled fists hid under the wings of her arms. "I'm not jumping out of this plane into the darkness alone!"

"Oh relax Alexandria." James laughed as the plane gently cruised into the night sky. "You're not jumping out of the plane at all. Especially since you were planning on using a life jacket instead of a parachute." Now unable to control his laugh, James was utterly hysterical.

Clearly embarrassed, Alexandria could do nothing but laugh as well. After all, she had been caught in her own web, something that almost never happened. Finally she said, "You know, Nicole warned me about pretending to be something I'm not."

"You should have taken her up on her warning," James replied in a tickled but very soothing voice. "Just sit back, relax and enjoy the ride Alexandria, because I have a surprise waiting for you."

As James and Alexandria arrived at his private beach, her eyes lit up as she observed hundreds of lit candles flickering in the night and guiding them up the runway. Once on the beach, much to Alexandria's surprise, there, facing the ocean, she found a beautiful white blanket also surrounded by candles. On top of the blanket, there sat a large picnic basket with a single pink rose lying on top of it with a note attached to it that read.

In honor of your first skydiving lesson ...

"You knew all along?" Alexandria asked. "But How?"

"How?" James asked. "Alexandria," he replied now laughing and shaking his head back and forth. "No one skydives at night."

The two laughed together as James grabbed Alexandria's hand to help her keep her balance as she sat on the beautifully prepared blanket where they spent the entire night talking, laughing and eating the best seafood, cheese, crackers and grapes ever tasted while drinking the best wine flown in from the great Napa Valley.

At six-o'clock am, James and Alexandria sat and watched the sun come up. A year later, the two were married at 6:00 am in Cancun on the same private beach facing the ocean, where they first fell in love.

Fourteen

As Alex and James continued their drive from the airport, James turned from the window towards Alex and said, "So, Alex, what have you been up to while I was away? I've been gone for three weeks, and I want to know how you survived without me."

Alex gave James a quick glance and laughed. "Well sweetie, where do you want me to start?"

"From the beginning baby," he replied.

"Ok," she laughed while trying to be serious. "The first week, I cried my eyes out because I missed my wonderful husband so much. The second week I cried."

"Alex!" James interrupted.

"What?" She chuckled as they both began to laugh. "I thought you wanted to know what I was doing while you were away?"

"Girl stop playing." He laughed and said, "You know what I'm talking about."

"Ok, ok," Alexandria laughed. "Don't get your pilot's drawers all in a bunch."

"Well," Alexandria said with a short sigh and a voice of real concern. "Nicole's trial has been really hard on her. Every night James, I sit and listen to her cry and rehash all the shit that trial is putting her through. She doesn't know it, but after she leaves our home or after I hang up the phone from speaking with her... James, all I can do is sit on our bed and just cry my eyes out for her. Of all the people in the world James, Nikki is the last person who should ever have to go through this sort of drama. I mean she is such a kind and fair person who would give you the shirt off her back without so much as a whimper."

Alexandria paused for a moment and spoke as if she were in a trance, not realizing the anger in her voice or the distant look in her eyes. "James," she said as he turned and noticed his wife's ghostly change. "You know, life's funny because I believe, when this case is over Nikki will be the one who will claim victory and not Triscope and when the time comes, *they* are all going to regret ever hurting her."

Then suddenly as if someone had snapped their fingers, Alexandria became cheerful again and began telling James about Sukenya's wedding.

"James," she laughed as she slapped her hand on the steering wheel. "Wait until you see Suk. Miss calm and mild mannered is about to loose it. It is simply hysterical, I mean the girl has realized planning a wedding is no joke, especially when you're from a large family who can't seem to agree on anything."

"Sukenya and Greg are trying to stay within a certain budget but that family of hers is putting her through the wringer. Guilt trips and all! What's even funnier, Sukenya has less than eight months before her wedding. Thank God she has Brandy to help keep her grounded."

"Speaking of Brandy, girlfriend thinks she's pregnant again. Can you believe it James?" She asked with a chuckle. "If she is, Brandy and Darius will have five mouths to feed! Can you imagine having five mouths to feed James, Can you?" Alexandria asked again, half laughing and half talking as she shook her head back and forth saying, "Five Kids?"

"Wow!"

"I don't know?"

"Whew!"

102

Then said loudly, "I wish them luck."

"I think Brandy and Darius are the lucky ones," James replied. "I mean you have to admit Alexandria, they are wonderful parents." James paused for a moment and asked, "Alexandria, why don't we think about starting a family?"

"Sure," Alexandria laughed. "Why don't we think about it?" Alexandria paused for a moment and said in a sarcastic tone, "I'll let you know when I have an answer."

Alex didn't see the hurt in James's eyes. He was serious, and so was she.

Fifteen

Three weeks later...

It had been three weeks since Brandy discovered a lump in her left breast while showering. At first, like most women, she thought maybe she was imagining what she felt. But after the second and then third self-examination, Brandy knew it was definitely a lump.

She immediately phoned her doctor who at first, brushed off Brandy's concern with, "All women have lumps in their breasts, especially right before their period when a woman's breasts are sometimes lumpy and very tender. It's probably nothing."

Brandy however, wasn't buying the doctor's theory.

At Brandy's persistence, her doctor scheduled an emergency examination and recommended she have a mammogram. While the x-ray showed nothing, a small voice inside wouldn't let Brandy accept the doctor's answer. Once again, at Brandy's request, her doctor referred her to a breast specialist, who scheduled a series of tests and ordered an ultrasound. After the ultrasound, the specialist closely analyzed the pictures where she noticed a small mass and scheduled a biopsy.

Twenty-four hours later, the doctor gave Brandy the grim news. The lump in her breast was indeed cancerous! Because of the size and location of the mass, the doctor suggested removing Brandy's entire left breast. Before agreeing to the surgery, Brandy went for a second and third opinion. each time, she was given the same option. A complete mastectomy...

And now three weeks later, Brandy and her husband Darius were in route to the hospital for a life altering surgery.

The ride to the hospital took two hours, which gave Brandy time to think. *"Three weeks ago,"* she quietly thought to herself, *"my main concern was Sukenya's wedding. Now, I'm on my way to a hospital two hours away from my babies to have one of my breasts removed. What I wouldn't give to really be pregnant,"* she sighed.

105

As a way to throw off her best friends, Brandy had fabricated her entire story about being pregnant. *"After all,"* she sighed again. *"How can I drop this on them now? With Sukenya planning her wedding and poor Nikki barely hanging on because of that horrible trial, the last thing I want to do, is burden them with this."*

Just then Darius placed his hand on top of Brandy's and gave her a comforting squeeze.

"Don't worry baby," he said. "It's going to be alright, I promise."

Strong and secure in his love for Brandy, Darius silently prayed, *"She's my life Lord. She's all I've ever needed and or wanted. I thank you for bringing her into my life and for allowing me to love her. She is the mother of my children who, through your blessings were allowed to come through her womb and bring to us a joy neither one of us could have ever imagined. So Lord, I beg of you, please, do not take her away from us...Please do not take her a way... from me!!!"*

Darius was scared, but he couldn't let Brandy see it.

As Brandy stared at Darius, she marveled at his presence. *Such a strong man,* she thought as her mind went back to her college days at Norfolk State. Where she first met and fell in love with Darius.

106

Brandy quietly smiled as she remembered one of her many conversations she'd had back then with her girlfriends concerning him.

"Hey Brandy," Sukenya, Alexandria, and Nicole teased. "Please tell us. What on earth do you see in Darius?" they asked. "He's such a nerd."

"A nerd," Brandy snapped. "You all wouldn't know a good man if he bent down, and bit you on the ass."

"Well what in the hell do you call all these damn marks?" Alexandria laughed as she lifted up the back of her skirt and pointed to her behind.

"Alexandria!" Brandy shrieked. "You are soooo crazy!"

Sukenya and Nicole put their hands over their mouths in awe of Alexandria's gesture but then let out a hysterical howl.

Brandy swallowed hard to keep the lump she felt forming in her throat down as she remembered her days of yesteryear, *when life was oh so simple.*

What Brandy saw in Darius so many years ago, was promise. Promise to love her fully. Promise to help her achieve some of life's dreams. Promise to see that while yes, he was somewhat nerdy he had great potential. Most of all, the promise to love her till death do us part, and even after that. The promise of her true soul mate.

107

"Darius," Brandy softly called out.

"Shush," Darius answered. "It's going to be all right. Just relax and focus on our future. Because this," he said, "is another test of our faith, a test that surely we are not going to fail. Remember our babies?" he asked. "Trust me Bran it is going to be all right."

Brandy leaned over and rested her head on his shoulder. As she closed her eyes, she thought to herself. *He always could read my mind.* as she remembered their very intimate encounter from the previous night.

Just twenty-four hours earlier, Darius had walked in on Brandy as she stood naked in front of their floor length bathroom mirror.

Brandy had been standing in front of her mirror for what seemed to be a lifetime. During that time, her eyes had traced every inch of her body. She stared at her face, her neck, her shoulders, her arms, her stomach, her round hips, and her very shapely legs. Never once, did she look at what she really needed to look at... Her breasts.

Finally, Brandy took a deep breath and stared straight at them. *Funny* she thought, but her breasts seemed to be staring right back at her. Brandy then began to speak to her breasts as if they could hear her.

"How could you do this to me," she asked out loud. "How? How could one of you let cancer creep into my body and not give me any warning?"

Brandy stared silently at her breasts as if she expected them to give her an answer. She then wondered if Darius would ever look at her the same. Suddenly, Brandy realized she wasn't alone. As she looked up, her eyes met her husband's. After fifteen years of marriage, she was used to Darius seeing her naked, but, for some strange reason, this time, she reached for her robe.

Anticipating her move, Darius grabbed her right hand and gently placed it into his, never once taking his eyes off of her eyes. He then slowly walked up behind Brandy and placed her left hand into his as he moved closer behind her. Darius was so close Brandy could feel his heart beating. Yet, he never said a word, nor did he take his eyes off of hers.

Instead, they both just stood there and stared into each other's eyes through their mirror.

They were transfixed. Darius remained silent as he slowly raised Brandy's right hand and gently placed it on her left breast. He then raised her left hand and gently placed it on her right breast.

As they stood there staring into each other's eyes through the mirror cradling her breasts, Darius finally whispered into his wife's right ear. "These are not the reasons why I fell in love and married you. Although your breasts are beautiful, they are beautiful not in spite of you, but rather, because of you. They are in no way, shape or form what makes you the woman that I've loved and cherished for over fifteen years."

"I love you Brandy because of your warm and generous heart and your free spirit. I love you because of your beautiful smile and your inviting laugh. I love you my dear wife, because of your ability to love without expecting anything in return. I love you most of all, because of your honest and trusting demeanor. You see, baby without you ..."

His voice began to crack *as* Darius slowly turned Brandy around so that they were now face-to-face staring deeply into each other's very watery eyes, *There would be no me.* I love you Brandy," he cried, "mind, body and soul."

Darius leaned over and gently kissed Brandy, first on her forehead then on her left cheek, her right cheek, and her nose. By the time Darius kissed Brandy on her lips, their tears blended together as one, which for the past 15 years is what they'd become. One mind. One body. One spirit. One spirit of love.

"Now," he laughed, trying to make light of the very serious situation. "If you were going to loose this..." Darius slowly moved his hands down and palmed Brandy's very round and firm behind. As he tilted his head to the side and playfully squeezed Brandy's buttocks while raising one of his very thick eyebrows and smiled as he said, "...Then we might have a problem."

"Forget you boy." Brandy laughed as she tried to pull away from Darius. But his embrace was too tight. He simply pulled her closer to him where they both gave each other a hug so tight, they could barely breathe.

"I love you baby," Darius humbly whispered.

"I love you too," Brandy tenderly replied.

That night, Brandy and Darius made the most beautiful love, the kind of love that was truly love of the spirit. "Flesh of my flesh, bone of my bone."

Sixteen

Although, Brandy's surgery wasn't scheduled until 9:30 am, Brandy and Darius arrived at the hospital at 6:00 am sharp. As the nurses prepared Brandy for surgery, she was a bundle of nerves.

"Don't be nervous," said one of the nurses as she helped Brandy into bed.

"That's right Brandy!" a familiar voice interrupted, "Don't be nervous."

Brandy looked up and her eyes immediately filled with tears, because to her surprise, in walked Sukenya, Nicole and Alexandria.

"What are you all doing here?" Brandy asked with a smile as bright as the sun.

"Girl you know your husband can't keep anything from us," replied Sukenya.

"Brandy we told you years ago," Alexandria laughed. "The man was a nerd!"

"Stop it Alex," scolded Nicole.

"Especially since I'm standing right here." Darius said in a joking manner.

The four women at first filled the room with laughter and then a dead silence fell upon the room.

Sukenya finally broke their silence. She walked over and took Brandy's trembling hand as she said, "Sweetie, this is just a test of faith from God. You and Darius have been through so much and have always come out on top. Just look at those beautiful babies. Believe in Jesus and Trust in God's will. Know that through him all things are possible. I love you girl and need you in my life more than you will ever know. Maybe that's selfish for me to say right now but it is the truth."

"Brandy," Nicole interrupted. "You are the glue that holds us together. Think of those beautiful babies and that wonderful husband of yours. We all need you. That's why I know we are going to get through this together."

Alexandria replied, "Well of course we'll get through this. I mean damn, it's a titty! Hell Bran, if you want you can have one of these big jugs," she laughed as she arched her back in a way that made her breasts poke out, "as long as ya leave me with a hand or shall I say a mouth full."

Brandy, Sukenya and Nicole stared at Alexandria with their mouths open and faces frowned. As Darius simply put his hand on his forehead and rocked his head back and forth.

"What???" Alexandria asked as she felt the sharp sting of their icy glares. "I made you all forget about the surgery didn't I?" she grinned.
Once again, the four friends filled the room with laughter.

As Brandy drifted off to sleep, she smiled and quietly said, "Thanks everyone for being here with me today. I love all of you sooo very, very much."

Darius leaned over his wife's bed and softly whispered into her ear, "We love you too baby, hurry back."

Six months later...

It's been six months since Brandy's surgery. Miraculously, the cancer had only settled in her left breast. As a precaution, during surgery the doctors also removed two of Brandy's lymph nodes, which, after extensive tests, showed no signs of cancer.

"Whew!" she shouted as Brandy let out a sigh of relief. "Thank you Jesus," she laughed, as the doctors gave her the good news. "Thank you for my life!"

Although, this was Brandy's first of many follow up visits, she felt confident that all would be well. Brandy turned and looked at her very happy husband, Darius and gave him a gigantic hug as she said, "Baby from this day forward we are going to live our lives to the fullest."

"Yes," a very grateful Darius replied, "with you by my side Brandy, my life will always be full." As Darius hugged his wife, he looked up to the heavens and also thanked God for their wonderful blessing. For Brandy had come out of the hospital ready and eager to resume her life.

"Darius I have so much to do," she said as the couple drove home with their wonderful news. "Sukenya's wedding is less than three months away and with Nicole's trial finally coming to an end, It is important that I'm there at the courthouse to give her my support."

Darius listened to Brandy ramble on and on about all of the things she had to take care of and smiled as he said, "Yeah, she's my life."

Seventeen

One Month Later...

G ood morning! It's 6:00am. What a great morning to start the rest of your life...

Alexandria opened one eye and looked at the alarm clock. Sure enough, the clock read 6:00 am, just as Doug and DeDe's voices had said. With a quick swing of her right hand, Alexandria attempted to hit the snooze button and missed. The radio continued blaring Doug and DeDe's voices saying, "get up everyone. Today is the first day of the rest of your life."

"I'm not ready to get up yet," Alexandria moaned out loud to the radio as if the radio personalities could hear her. "Just twenty more minutes...Just twenty more minutes, that's all I need..."

Alexandria turned over on her back, and took a deep breath as she stared blankly at the ceiling.

"Damn," she sighed. "I can't believe I didn't get home until four o'clock this morning. What was I thinking about?" she said, as she tapped her forehead. "Whew! It's a good thing James is on a one-month flight path overseas, or else, my ass would be in deep shit right about now. Ugggg," she sighed as she sat up, swung her legs over her bed, tumbled out and moaned, "I'm definitely getting too old for this crap, but damn was last night one for the books."

As Alexandria showered, she thought about her late night, early morning rendezvous and began to laugh. "What a poor sick ass. I know I'm giving him the best sex he's ever known, but this is nothing more than a business deal. Furthermore, I can't believe he wants me to leave my husband and move into his penthouse just so that I can be closer to him. Now that's what I call whipped." She laughed out loud and said, "What a joke!" as she then began to recite verbatim her lover's words to her from the night before.

"I love you Alexandria, I want to be with you every chance I get. If it weren't for my wife's fortune, I'd leave her ass tomorrow. I've never loved her," he

117

pleaded. "I've never loved anyone the way I love you. Won't you please reconsider my offer?"

"Yeah I got your offer," Alexandria said in a dry voice as she stepped out of her shower patted herself dry and draped herself in her favorite robe. Suddenly, Alexandria heard her doorbell ring. *Now who could that be at this time of the morning,* she asked herself as she walked towards her front door. It was Brandy.

"Good morning Brandy, what has you up so early?" Alexandria asked as she let Brandy into her house.

"You!" Brandy replied as she walked pass Alexandria and towards the kitchen. "You and your never-ending schemes."

"Oh, brother," Alexandria mumbled as she followed Brandy into her kitchen. "What have I done now?" She asked in a dry tone as she placed her hand under her chin and leaned on the kitchen counter top.

"What have you done?" Brandy squawked, as she pulled out several hotel receipts from her pocketbook and flung them on top of Alexandria's kitchen counter as she piercingly asked,

"What in the hell are you doing?"
Brandy had recently stumbled upon several hotel receipts inadvertently left in a pocketbook Alexandria

had borrowed from her months ago and realized that Alexandria was secretly having an affair.

"Alexandria now you know, that I know for a fact James was not in town during any of these dates. And how do I know?" Brandy asked Alexandria as well as answered. "Because he called me from various countries while I was in the hospital. Alex, how can you cheat on James? And why would you want to? I mean he's the best thing that has ever come into your life. Damn Alexandria!" Brandy continued. "I thought you had given up that crap in college. But I guess a leopard never changes her spots. Does she?"

Alexandria finally replied by simply saying, "Brandy my little outside recreation, is not as deep as you think. As far as I am concerned, I'm not cheating on my husband. I love him with all of my heart. Besides, this guy is simply something to do while James is away. And the fact that he's rich and powerful helps me to remember just how much I love my husband. Trust me Brandy," Alex pleaded. "I know what I'm doing!"

"Does Nicole know about this?" Brandy quietly asked.

"Why in the hell would I tell Nicole?" Alexandria snapped. "She's not my keeper."

"You're right Alexandria she is not your keeper, but she is worried about you. She says you are forever disappearing when James is out of town and that you've never once stepped foot into the courthouse to show her your support."

"And that constitutes me cheating?" Alexandria chuckled. "Perhaps you and my dear sweet cousin should focus on her trial and stay out of my business. After all, she is the one trying to prove a case, not me."

"Alex, how can you joke about something so serious?" Brandy snapped. "Nicole is fighting for her life, and the best answer you can come up with is stay out of your business? Hell, if it weren't for Nicole, you wouldn't have a business. Alexandria, Nicole is your first cousin who is and has always been there for you. Don't you think it is about time you did something for her? I mean Friday is Nicole's last day in court, and after three and a half grueling years it would be nice for you to finally show up. Because it doesn't look good for Nicole."

Brandy spoke in a serious and concerned tone as she slowly shook her head back and forth and rubbed her hands together. "Not good at all." Brandy took a deep breath and looked up at Alexandria with tears in her eyes and said, "Alex she is going to need a miracle to pull this off and we all need to be there for her."

Alexandria quietly replied, "Brandy, I already promised Nikki, that I would be there for her on Friday. She doesn't have to worry because this time I'll be there."

Eighteen

Today's morning session began like all the others before. However, today's session was different. Different because today was Nicole's final day in court. After three and a half years and numerous testimonies, her case was finally coming to an end. But once again, the employees of Triscope marched into the courtroom and denounced Nicole's entire case. According to them, Nicole and no one else witnessed Tom's reign of terror. According to them, it was Sheila who transgressed against Nicole. Sheila and only Sheila.

After listening to this kind of rhetoric for what seemed to be an eternity, Nicole leaned over to her attorney and asked, "Are they really that afraid of Tom? How can they sit in a courtroom and lie the way they are doing? What does Tom have on them?"

she asked as she stared blankly into her attorney's eyes. Nicole's voice began to tremble as she continued talking. "After all of this time, I am going to lose aren't I Chris? ... I am! I'm..."

"Shush, Nicole," Chris interrupted and whispered, "Where is your faith? Now is not the time for you to break down. Just hold on a little longer. Besides, we've come too far to lose now."

"You're right Chris. Now is not the time for me to break down. Actually, NOW IS THE TIME FOR ME TO TESTIFY AND TELL THE GOD DAMN TRUTH!" she screamed

The Judge, paying absolutely no attention to Nicole's outburst, banged his gavel once and said, "The court will now take one hour for lunch. Oh and Mr. Bellows," the judge cautioned. "I advise you to restrain your client before this afternoon's session begins." The Judge banged his gavel and announced, "Lunch is now in session."

During Lunch, Nicole pleaded with her attorney to let her testify.

In the past, Chris had recommended that Nicole not take the witness stand for fear of Triscope's attorneys twisting Nicole's entire testimony around thereby causing more harm to her case then good.

Nicole agreed with her attorney and instead allowed others to testify on her behalf. But today after three and a half years of listening, Nicole had a change of heart.

"Chris," she cried. "If I'm going to lose this case, at least let me tell my side of the story. This is my life, and I must do this for me. If no one ever believes me, at least I'll know I told the truth. At least I'll know that I was able to look Tom and the rest of those arrogant bastards in their eyes and show them. You may have tried to break me, but you only made me stronger. Do you hear me Chris?" Nicole asked, but he didn't respond. "Chris, are you listening?"

"Yes Nicole," he slowly replied. "I heard you." Chris was listening, but he seemed preoccupied.

After much deliberation, Nicole got her chance to sit on the witness stand and tell her side of the story. Twice she broke down and sobbed. But Nicole told her side of the story.

For Nicole, telling her side of the story meant more than actually winning the case. It was in her mind of reasoning, a self-healing process to once and for all release the anger and move on with her life. After all, she now had a company of her own to run.

Nicole's testimony genuinely moved the jurors. Sadly, though, it was her word against numerous other testimonies fervently telling just the opposite of her story.

To make matters worse, during Nicole's cross-examination, Triscope's attorney tore Nicole's testimony to shreds, often, badgering Nicole by saying, "Admit it Nicole. The only reason why you are seeking revenge on Triscope is because Sheila, Tom's former secretary and culprit who actually framed you, is dead."

Sheila had been mysteriously killed in a hit and run accident two weeks after being released from prison.

"No, that's not right!" Nicole replied. "It wasn't just Sheila, It was Tom who... "

"Save your remarks Nicole and just answer the questions yes or no," Triscope's attorney growled.

"But..." Nicole tearfully continued. "It was Tom who hurt me. It was Tom who tried to sabotage an important deal I had with Sintech. It was Tom who tried to minimize my role as a woman and as an employee at Triscope. It was Tom who told me to go home and make babies."

"Liar!" Triscope's attorney yelled at Nicole's face as he knowingly allowed saliva to fly from his mouth. "It was Sheila who caused you to breakdown Nicole. Sheila!" He yelled again. "Sheila and not Tom!"

"I object your honor!!" Chris interrupted in a loud and agitated voice. "Sir, he is clearly badgering my client."

The judge nonchalantly looked over at Nicole and said in a dry tone, "Over-ruled."

"Thank you your honor, I have no further questions anyway," Triscope's attorney said as he looked over at Nicole with a slight grin, and walked away.

It was relatively obvious to Nicole that her case of three and a half years and two hundred thousand dollars in attorney fees was quickly coming to an end. An end to what began as an attempt to disclose all of Tom's discriminating and unfair labor practices towards his employees.

Fueled by anger, yes. Revenge, yes. And the sincere desire to once again make Triscope the wonderful company she had began her career at some fifteen years ago with a wonderfully fair but now deceased man named Fred.

Nicole looked up from the witness stand barely able to focus through her tears. She was, however, able to see Tom, members of his board and the actual owner of Triscope laughing and celebrating their imminent victory. Nicole then looked over and saw Chris who had such a look of sorrow in his eyes as he silently mouthed to her, "Don't give up."

Nicole continued to scan the room until she spotted Brandy and Sukenya who were sitting together with tears streaming down their cheeks.

"Where's Alexandria?" she asked herself as she quietly mumbled, "In the past three and a half years in which I've fought this battle, my cousin has never once stepped foot into this courtroom. How could Alex not show up after she promised me she'd be here for me today? Perhaps she knew that I was going to lose and decided it would be best to simply stay away. Which is what I should have done." Nicole then broke into an uncontrollable sob.

Chris immediately stood up and said, "Your Honor, I would like to ask for a ten-minute recess to allow my client to compose herself."

Triscope's attorney quickly stood and said with a loud and self-assured voice. "Your Honor, It's been a very trying time for everyone. Can we please just get this over with and go right into closing arguments?"

"Your Honor!" interrupted Chris in a loud voice. "Sir, please, with all due respect, I am only asking for a ten-minute recess so that my client can compose herself. Surely ten minutes is not going to cause any damage to this case!"

Finally, the judge said. "I'll give you your ten minutes Mr. Bellows, but I'm putting you on notice, my patience is running thin."

As Nicole walked off the witness stand, she felt numb as hundreds of questions raced back and forth within her mind.

"Why is Tom getting away with this?" she asked. "How Lord can they set out to destroy me, one of your own and then get away with it? Please help me to understand this!" she silently pleaded.

Nicole walked towards her attorney and collapsed into his arms and again began to sob uncontrollably. "I... I... I thought that I had gotten over this," she sobbed. "I thought with God and the truth on my side, how could I lose? How?" she cried. "How could I lose?"

Chris gently held Nicole and whispered into her ear, "We're not going to lose! I told you in the beginning Nicole, we were going to win this case, and we will. You just have to trust me on this!" "OK?" he asked as he looked into her very red watery eyes.
Nicole nodded her head in agreement and began to walk out of the courtroom.

As Chris and Nicole walked towards the courtroom doors, Nicole turned and gave Brandy and Sukenya a halfhearted smile.

"We love you girl." chimed both women.

"It's going to be all right," whispered Brandy.

"You, see Nicole," Chris leaned over and whispered as they exited the courtroom. "Even Brandy and Sukenya know that everything is going to be all right!"

"Funny," she quietly thought, *"but there is something in the way Chris is talking that makes me really feel that I can believe him..."*

Nineteen

"Damn, I can't believe I broke my heel. How could this happen to me again? I know," Alexandria laughed while shaking her head back and forth and waving her hands in the air. "It's a conspiracy. First with James and now Nicole, except this time my shoe breaks while I'm trying to get to the courthouse! Oh my God!" she squealed. "It is 12 o'clock noon. Nikki is going to kill me! I know I promised her I'd be there today, but sorry Nik, I have to stop at the Mall first. Because, I cannot walk into the courtroom looking hit! I know my number one cousin will understand. She always has." Alexandria nervously laughed. "Besides, how long can it take to buy one pair of shoes?"

Twenty

It was now 3 o'clock in the afternoon and Nicole's ten-minute recess was over. Nicole was a bundle of nerves. She wasn't sure what Chris had up his sleeve, but she knew it was something, because, during their ten-minute recess, Chris had made several phone calls on his cell phone, never once explaining to Nicole what he was doing or to whom he was talking to.

Nicole and Chris sat in their chairs as the judge banged his gavel and said. "Court is now in sess..."

Before the judge could finish his sentence, the courtroom doors opened, and in walked Alexandria. Alexandria was a very beautiful and shapely five foot eleven-- One hundred and forty pounds woman. She had gorgeous long curly blond hair with the most unbelievable tropical ocean blue green eyes. Because of her flawless light complexion, she was often mistaken to be a woman of European decent when in reality she was an African American.

When they were children, Nicole often protected Alexandria from other children who, at times, didn't quite understand why she looked European although her parents were black. Especially when she relaxed her naturally curly blond hair. Today, as she entered the courtroom, her hair was curly.

Alexandria proceeded to walk towards the front of the courtroom towards Nicole, first passing Sukenya and Brandy, who simply laughed and shook their heads as they said, "Well at least she's here."

Once Alexandria reached the area where Nicole was sitting, she leaned over and whispered, "Nicole, I am so sorry I'm late, but girl you will not believe what happened to me…"

Suddenly, the CEO and owner of Triscope; Mr. Sam Burgess, stood up and started shouting. "Your Honor. I can't take this anymore. Your Honor, I'd like to confess."

Tom leaned over and pulled the side of Mr. Burgess's coat jacket and snarled between his teeth. "Sit down Sam! What in the hell do you think you're doing?" he growled as he attempted to pull the man back into his chair.

"Let go of me!" Mr. Burgess yelled. "I'm doing what I should have done a long time ago. I'm telling the truth! Your honor, my name is Mr. Sam Burgess. I am the owner of Triscope. Tom and Triscope are guilty of all charges. Everything that poor woman has been saying is true. What Tom did to her is unforgivable. I should have put a stop to his shenanigans years ago," he continued, now visibly shaken. "But Tom threatened to kill my wife and I if I ever said anything. He said he could and would make our deaths look like a mysterious accident."

"Wha, what!" a surprised Tom shouted. "What did you just say?"

"Order in the court!" the Judge yelled as he banged his gavel. Bang! Bang! Bang! "Order in the court!" But there was no order.
Tom was now standing and waving his fists in Mr. Burgess's face with a look of unbelievable anger and hatred in his eyes.

"There is no way in Hell you are going to pin this shit on me Sam!" he shouted. "No way in Hell! If I go down buddy, you can best believe, you're going down with me!! After all, you're the one who hired me remember? You're the one who hand picked me to get rid of Nicole. And why Nicole?" He yelled as he turned towards her and for the first time in three and a half years stared straight into Nicole's eyes. "Because Sam resented the fact that Nicole had brains, good looks and could not be bought. Sam also knew of Nicole's good heart and strong mind. He knew Nicole was loyal to her former and now deceased boss named Fred. Who was also Sam's wife's only brother and true owner of Triscope!"

"What!" Sam yelled. "That's bullshit! You're the one, Tom, who openly discussed Nicole's fate in a board meeting, and," he laughed, "I have it all on tape!" Sam was now laughing and waving a tiny cassette as Tom's eyes froze with fear.

"You didn't!" Tom said in a surprised and bewildered voice.

"Order in the court!" the Judge yelled once again as he banged his gavel. Bang! Bang! Bang! "Order in the court!"

Finally, there was silence.

The judge then said. "Mr. Burgess and Mr. Jackovich. With all due respect, will you both pleeeze sit down? In all my years as a judge, I have never seen anything like this."

The judge then ordered both men, their attorneys, and Chris into his chambers.

Alexandria was now sitting next to Brandy and Sukenya who, like Nicole, Chris and the entire

Triscope team merely stared at Mr. Burgess and Tom in utter disbelief.

"*Who was telling the truth?*" they all wondered.

Was Mr. Burgess simply having a nervous breakdown or had Sam really hired Tom to get rid of Nicole?

As the men entered the judge's chambers, Nicole turned to her friends and made a facial gesture while raising one eyebrow. "What just happened?" she mouthed to the three women.

The women wordlessly hunched their shoulders in unison and shook their heads back and forth.

Nicole then turned back around and placed her face into her hands. Quietly, she said, "I cannot believe this is happening. After three and a half years and two hundred thousand dollars in court fees, my case has just come down to not only my word against Tom's, but also the owner's words against Tom's. Is this man really confessing?" she asked herself, "or is he simply having a nervous breakdown? I don't know," she silently prayed while rubbing her forehead, "but if he is having a breakdown, please God, please let the judge believe him, before he does."

Twenty One

It has been four hours since the judge ordered the men into his chambers. For Nicole, it has been four hours of silence. Four long hours of wondering... *What is going on in there?*

As Nicole quietly sat in the courtroom waiting for Chris to resurface, she tried to digest what had occurred earlier. She wondered why would Mr. Burgess, whom she'd only met once or twice, confess, especially since the case was going in their favor. *"Had he really hired Tom to destroy me?"* she asked. *"If so, then why? And what did Tom mean when he said, "I couldn't be bought?"*

Nicole moaned as she massaged her temples and said out loud, "If only I knew what was going on in the judges chambers!" She then looked back to check and see if her friends were still there. Brandy, Sukenya and Alexandria were sitting in the same seats they'd taken four hours earlier.

However, Alexandria's head bobbed up and down as she caught a quick nap.

"That girl will sleep anywhere," Nicole laughed.

Just then, the doors to the judge's chambers opened and out walked the men. Chris had a blank look on his face, but seemed to have floated to his chair.

Humph, Nicole thought to herself. *In all the time Chris has been representing me, I never realized how fine he was! His honey colored complexion, almond shaped deep kohl colored eyes and black curly hair, never once crossed my mind. Humm...he sort of reminds me of that basketball player Rick Fox.*

As Chris sat down in his chair, he grabbed Nicole's hand and gave it a comforting squeeze.

Damn his hands are as soft as cotton...

The judge banged his gavel once and said, "Court is now in session." The jurors were the first of whom the judge addressed.

"Although this has been a very long and emotional trial, I would like to personally thank each and every one of you for your sacrifice and dedication in this matter. I would also like to thank you for sitting and listening to countless testimonies from numerous witnesses. I would like to thank you for selflessly giving up three and a half years of your life which, at times included being away from your families and being away from your friends, being away from your husbands and being away from your wives. Although," he paused and chuckled, "some of you considered that a break."

The jury quietly smiled at his warm joke.

"But most of all," he continued, now serious again, "being away from your children. Missing birthdays, missing games and missing them. Never once did any of you complain. Never once, did any of you show signs of fatigue. Your patience and sincere desire to serve for truth and justice is to be truly commended. However," he said as he cleared his throat. "In lieu of today's events, you are all dismissed."

As the members of the jury walked off the stand, the courtroom hummed with a slight commotion. The judge, however, ignored the sound and focused all of his attention on Nicole. Once he called her name, the courtroom fell silent …

"Nicole, will you please stand?" he asked.

Nicole and Chris both rose together. As Nicole began to rise, her knees buckled underneath her.

Chris, being the charismatic attorney that he was, anticipated her reaction and grabbed her under her elbow before anyone could see her sway. The weight of his hand, gave Nicole the extra strength she needed in order to stand and face the judge with confidence.

"However this goes," she calmly said to herself. "I have the victory!"

As the judge began to address Nicole, she noticed his blank but very stern facial expression.

In preparation to anesthetize herself from his words, Nicole inhaled all of the air her lungs could hold and released it very slowly.

"Nicole," he said, "you my dear are a pillar for justice. Day after day, you were ridiculed and called a liar. Day after day, you professed Triscope's actions to be true while numerous testimonies said otherwise. Day after day, based on the testimonies brought before me, I'd often say, this woman doesn't have a chance in hell of winning this case. For three and a half years Nicole, day after day, that was the scenario..."

The judge paused and stared deep into Nicole's eyes, a stare that made Nicole's heart began to pound hard and fast, loud and fast. Faster and faster until the sound of her heart beating totally engulfed her.

"But Nicole," he smiled, "today is not like any of those days."

What? What did he just say? Nicole asked herself as the sound of her pounding heart disappeared.

"Because today Nicole is the day that your conviction, dedication and determination comes to fruition. Today is your day for justice! Today is your day for victory! Today is the day you receive both closure and peace as you step into the first day of the rest of your life!"

The judge cleared his throat and continued his speech.

"Triscope has pleaded guilty to all charges and has agreed to not only reimburse you for all of your legal fees, but to also award you for all of your pain and suffering: *one billion tax-free dollars*. To be paid to you immediately. Your attorney has your check. Nicole, while I personally believe that there is no amount of money to ever replace the pain caused by these people, this I believe, will surely help ease some of your symptoms. With that said, court is now dismissed."

The judge banged his gavel and ended the three and a half year discrimination case.

As the judge retired to his chambers, he stopped short at his door, turned around and gave Nicole the thumbs up sign and quickly disappeared as the doors closed behind him.

***

Two hours later...

"One billion dollars!" Nicole screamed. "One billion dollars! Chris, please tell me again so that I know I'm not dreaming. Did the judge really say I was awarded one billion dollars?"

"It's no dream Nicole," Chris replied as they turned up the driveway to her home. "You were awarded one billion dollars. Dang Nicole." he laughed. "I showed you the check three times before we left the courthouse."

"And," Alexandria interrupted as they walked into Nicole's house. "You stared at the check all the way here!"

"I know," Nicole laughed, "I know, but this is sooo unbelievable! God is Good," she laughed, "God is oh so good!"

"Yes He is!" Brandy and Sukenya agreed and laughed as they said in sequence, "Nicole, In addition to you winning an astonishing settlement, we are all dying to know what happened."

"So am I!" Nicole shrieked with excitement. "So am I! Because I'm standing here holding a check for one billion dollars and I still don't know what happened. I mean why would the company settle? Especially when they were on the verge of winning. I don't get it," she said as she plopped down on her sofa. "Chris, do you have any idea?" a puzzled but overwhelmed Nicole asked. "Please tell me Chris," Nicole pleaded. "Please tell me what happened while you were in the judge's chambers?"

"Yeah Chris," Alexandria interrupted. "Please tell us what happened. I mean why would a company deny Nicole's charges for three and a half years and then suddenly admit their guilt. It was as if the owner, what was his name again?" Alexandria asked, as she snapped her finger and squinted up her face in an attempt to remember his name. "Had diarrhea of the mouth!"

"Sam," Nicole quietly answered. "His name is Sam Burgess, a man who before the trial, I'd only seen twice before. Once before Fred died and again at Fred's memorial service. Otherwise," she said as she stretched out her hands and hunched her shoulders, "I've never had any other kind of contact with him."

"Chris?" The three women all asked in harmony. "Did Tom really threaten Mister Burgess's life?"

"Or was he really the mastermind behind setting me up?" Nicole quietly asked.

"Beats me," Chris replied, as he poured each women a glass of Champagne. "The two men are definitely hiding something," he said. "But what, I don't know. Tom blamed the entire ordeal on Mr. Burgess and Sheila. Mr. Burgess however, claimed that Tom was the mastermind and that he simply went along with the setup because he feared for his life. Bottom line Nicole, they are both guilty by their own admission of trying to destroy you, but as far as admitting to who's telling the truth, you may never know. Because the two men instead agreed to pay all your legal fees and to settle your claim for an astonishing uncontested one billion dollars. So Nicole my strong and determined client," Chris smiled as he walked towards her and handed her a glass of champagne, "what started out as a nightmare has ended like that of a wonderful dream come true. So I guess we'll have to start calling you Oprah's little sister," he jokingly said.

"Now that would be an honor and a dream come true," Nicole teased.

Chris and Nicole's crystal glasses softly tapped. The ping of the two crystals meeting together sounded as if they were singing with victory.

"Drink up ladies," he laughed. "Drink up."

So, after three and a half long tormenting years, Nicole had finally won her case.

Twenty Two

It has been one month since Nicole won the largest settlement in the history of any discrimination suit. Because of her very public trial and enormous court settlement, Nicole was thrown into instant celebrity status. News reporters, talk shows and long lost relatives, were constantly bombarding her.

"My God Chris! What am I going to do?" she asked during one of their many phone conversations since her trial ended. "I thought after the trial, I was finally going to be able to get some rest. But that is far from what has happened, what do you think I should do?"

Nicole never realized how dependant she'd become on Chris. She valued his opinion more than she'd ever admit. Lately, when he was around, she considered him more of a friend than her attorney.

Chris listened to Nicole go on and on about how tired she was and how busy she was at work, and how because of the constant new pressures being placed on her she was unable to concentrate. To be honest, he actually enjoyed listening to her.

Nicole is such a beautiful person, he thought. *If ever anyone deserved justice for what those bastards put her through, it was Nicole.* "Nicole," Chris finally interrupted. "Why don't you take a trip?"

"A trip?" she asked.

"Yes," he replied. "After three and a half long mentally and physically draining years, Nicole, you need to get away and relax for a while."

"Chris," Nicole huffed, "I can't take a trip I have a company to run."

"Oh please Nicole," he laughed, "I think the company can run a couple of weeks without you. And, if it will make you feel any better, I will keep an eye on things until you return."

Chris could hear Nicole thinking over the phone because of the dead silence and her steady breathing. He hadn't realized how much his feelings for Nicole had become more personal than the traditional client-lawyer relationship. Lately, when he was around her he considered himself more of a friend than an attorney.

Well It would be nice to lie on the beach and get some rays, Nicole thought. *Lord knows I need it,* she silently laughed. *I know Alexandria would be down for some sun. She always is. Brandy has completed all of her cancer treatments, so I know the ocean's peacefulness would do her justice. And Sukenya, well with today being three days shy of her one month countdown before her wedding, girlfriend needs a break! But how,* Nicole pondered, *can I leave my company?*

Finally Chris could not take the dead silence any more and jokingly said, "Girl will you stop brain-fucking the idea and just do it!"

"What did you just say Chris?"

"You heard me," he laughed. "You called and asked for my opinion. I gave you an answer and you're going back and forth with yourself on what you should do. So consider my comment a free shock treatment to get your butt in gear."

The two laughed in agreement.

"Well Chris, your shock treatment has definitely worked!" Nicole laughed. "So Chris my good fellow," she jokingly said, "hold down the fort, because my girls and I are on our way to beautiful St. Thomas!!!"

Nicole did not have a hard time convincing the "girls" into taking a three-week all expense paid trip

147

to the Virgin Islands. "After all, thanks to Tom, Mr. Burgess and Triscope, I am a billionaire ya know!" she laughed, as she called each friend one by one saying "you ladies cannot pass up three weeks of tropical joy.

Brandy it is Wednesday morning and you only have three days to prepare, but trust me when I say, don't worry about your babies," she laughed, "because, between Darius, James, Greg and yes girl even Chris, your babies will be just fine. Just think of it as four men and four babies!"

"Lord help the men!" the two women laughed.

"To top it off, Bran, I've also hired the best nanny that money can buy. She comes highly recommended with lots of child rearing experience. Oh and Brandy, no need to worry, the woman is well over sixty, because now a days the fifty year olds aren't looking all that bad."

The two women laughed and squealed with excitement as they screamed, "St. Thomas here we come!"

"Sukenya, I know your wedding is one month away. No need to worry though, because everything has been taken care of. Trust me girl," Nicole laughed, "right down to the last stitch on your wedding gown and shoes."

"Shoes?" Sukenya asked. "I haven't been able to find the perfect pair yet."

"Yes I know." Nicole said. "That's why I'm having a shoe-maker flown in from Italy to personally design and hand-make your shoes to match your dress."

"Oh no you're not Nikki!" an elated Sukenya shouted.

"Yes I am girl!" Nicole laughed, "as a matter of fact, he should be at your door any minute."

"What!" Sukenya screamed, as she heard her doorbell ring.

"Oh yeah...One more thing Sukenya, I've also hired four additional coordinators to help you complete any last minute details you may have forgotten. Cinderella," Nicole laughed, "when you walk down the aisle, not only will you be the most beautiful bride on the East Coast, you'll also have a fresh St. Thomas tan to enhance your beautiful glow!"

The two women laughed and squealed with excitement as they screamed, "St. Thomas here we come!"

"Alexandria, after my courtroom fiasco, I shouldn't take you anywhere. How could you go shopping for a new pair of shoes on my most important day in court?" Nicole asked.

"Can I help it if my shoe broke?" Alexandria laughed. "Besides, all hell didn't break loose until after I arrived. And you have to admit Nicole," Alexandria laughed, "that, my dear cousin, was some crazy shit!"

"That's because Alexandria whenever you are around anything can and usually does happen!"

"That's my purpose in life." Alexandria laughed in a sarcastic tone. "That is, to keep everyone else on their toes!!"

"Whatever Miss Twinkle toes," Nicole laughed. "Whatever." Nicole paused for a moment and then said. "Okay Alexandria, let me see how fast you can dance around and pack your best string bikini and sun tan lotion."

"Because!" the two women laughed and squealed with excitement as they screamed,
"St. Thomas here we come!"

Twenty Three

After giving the ladies three days to prepare for their trip, Nicole chartered a private plane to fly them to St. Thomas. As they flew over the island, the women oohed and aahed at the picture perfect site of the white sandy beaches, beautiful flowers and crystal clear tropical blue ocean.

As the plane landed and the women exited the plane, they were greeted by the warm sun, beautiful island music and a continuous flow of tropical exotic island punch.

"Girls," Nicole laughed while sipping on her second drink. "We are about to have the best three weeks that money can buy, starting with that beautiful white stretch Mercedes limo parked over there waiting so patiently for us. For the next three weeks," she continued as the women walked towards the limo, "this will be our only means of transportation."

As the women entered the limo, Alexandria stepped back and snickered, "Well all righty then!" while lowering her sunglasses to get a better look at the very dark, fine and stocky chauffeur packing the women's luggage into the limo's trunk. "Ump, Ump, Ump," Alexandria wickedly laughed as she tilted her head to get a better look. "Not bad," she said. "Not bad at all."

The brother was neatly dressed in a pair of white shorts that showed off his very muscular thighs, with a black muscle t-shirt exposing his sculptured six-pack, strong biceps and powerful triceps, while a pair of black leather sandals rested at the end of his very strong stallion-like legs. His thick, well-manicured hands mechanically lifted their luggage. As his sexy smile exposed a set of beautiful white teeth when he paused and said in a deep voice, "Hello ladies, Welcome to beautiful St. Thomas."

The women giggled and said in unison like a bunch of silly pre-teens with high pitched out of tune voices, "Hello."

Brandy smiled as she quickly glanced over at Alexandria and said, "Put your claws in Alexandria.

P-u-t- cha claws in," she repeated in a slow dry voice. "And let me get a peek!"

The driver closed the door and the women all cracked up laughing as the limo pulled off.

"Whew!" Brandy laughed. "It's a good thing I'm married with four babies at home. Because if I wasn't that brother would be in some serious trouble right about now."

"Yeah, right Brandy," Sukenya jokingly said, "If that fine brother would have said 'boo' to you, girl you know you would have taken off like a bat out of hell!"

The women screamed with laughter as they gave each other high fives.

"Oh shut up Suk," Nicole teased. "You're not any better!"

"Well Excuse me Miss Thang," Sukenya laughed. "But I wasn't the one looking."

"Then how did you know the brother was fine Sukenya?" Nicole asked in an outrageously funny voice.

Once again, the women cracked up laughing as Sukenya shook her head and said. "Good one Nikki, good one, besides, I do have to admit. Good Lord the brother is fine!!"

"And," Alexandria squealed in a high-pitched voice, "he is our chauffeur for the next three weeks. My. My. My," she laughed. "This is going to be one hell of a trip!"

By now, the limo was going around a very steep winding hill and the women were feeling a little buzz from the island punch they had consumed at the airport. This feeling combined with their excitement of being *'free'* caused the women to start singing, "Hip hop hooray, ho, hey, ho," and they ended up singing, "We are family, I got all my sisters with me."

Within moments, the limo pulled up to the gate of an enormously elaborate and secluded fifteen-room villa.

Because the villa sat at the top of a mountain overlooking the ocean, the women had to, upon exciting the limo, walk down a flight of stairs just to enter the house. To their surprise, once they arrived at the bottom of the stairs, there stood four tall, dark and very handsome men to greet them.

"Welcome ladies," one of them said and smiled. "We're here to be at your every beck and call. If there is anything you ladies need and or desire, please do not hesitate to ask. My name is KiKi. This is Jason, Bobby and Ty."

With that, he clapped his hands twice and the doors of the villa slowly opened.

154

The women entered the immaculate house one by one and observed the foyer of their new living quarters.

"Oh damn," they all said as they placed their hands over their mouths in amazement. "Will you look at this place?"

To the right of where the women stood was a great living room filled with an exotic collection of marble pillars surrounded by glass, windows, mirrors and beautiful European furniture throughout the giant room. To the left of the room was a dining room filled with white marble furniture and a beautiful arrangement of flowers.

As the women walked towards the balcony to see what was below, to their surprise, they observed an olympic size swimming pool sitting right inside the house!

"Yes ladies I know," KiKi said in a self-assuring voice, "If I must say so myself, this place is 'the bomb'."

"Nicole, how did you ever find this place?" Alexandria asked in a high-pitched voice.

"Chris recommended it to me," she replied.

"Oh really!" Brandy laughed.

"I guess Chris also recommended these sugar bears too?" Sukenya whispered.

155

The women quietly snickered but KiKi heard Sukenya's comment and said, "Well excuse me Missy, we may be sugar bears to you, but to others, we're like Tony The Tiger. We're great!"

The three other men all snapped their fingers in agreement.

"Besides," KiKi smiled, "Chris is my first cousin on my father's side, who loves and accepts me for who I am."

"Oh KiKi, I'm sorry," Nicole laughed. "We were just having a little harmless fun that's all. We didn't mean any harm."

"None taken," Ty answered. "You ladies are here to have a good time. So I want you all to laugh, tease, scream and holla. Just so long as you have a good time. That's what KiKi promised Chris he'd do for each and every one of you. That is, to make sure you ladies have a great time. Do ya hear me ladies? I mean are y'all feelin me?"

"Um hum," the women replied while moving their heads up and down.

With that being said, KiKi motioned the men to escort the women to their double king sized master suites.

Sukenya, Brandy, Alexandria and Nicole systematically followed the men upstairs to four corners of the ten thousand square foot house. When they entered their bedrooms, their eyes lit up as they each scanned their one thousand square foot bedroom.

Each room was creatively decorated with an island flow. Along with a sunken sitting room, a European gas fireplace and an entertainment center strategically built into the length of an entire wall as French doors led out to a circular balcony overlooking the ocean. The rooms were surrounded by glass windows and high vaulted ceilings with sensor driven ceiling fans that hung high over a king size bed, which sat two feet off of the floor.

Mirrors surrounded each bathroom with glass vases strategically placed inside all four corners of the marbled walls and filled with an amazingly beautiful arrangement of freshly cut tropical flowers. In the center of it all, sat a Jacuzzi bathtub the size of a miniature pool. The glass circular walk in shower was big enough to accommodate four people and contained jet streams that came from all sections. No spots would be missed when you stepped into this setup. And last but not least the women observed a separate and private urinal for him and a French bidet for her.

The men led the women out of their bedrooms and continued giving them a tour of their beautiful island getaway. Which also included a winding staircase leading outside to a manmade tropical dream. Once outside, the women found a secluded enclave with an Olympic sized peanut shaped swimming pool, flanked by a swim up bar and an attached man-made waterfall, surrounded by tropical trees and flowers; thereby providing an awesome effect of total peace and tranquility.

"For the next three weeks ladies we will be your cooks, housecleaners, hairdressers, makeup artists and givers of your daily body massages from head to toe," KiKi cheerfully announced. "With the first of many massages beginning in 15 minutes."

"Oh Lord," the women all squealed as they ran up to their bedrooms to change. "If I'm dreaming, please don't ever think about waking me up!!!"

The women received their first of many massages outside on the patio of their tropical dream escape while sipping island punch and listening to the hum of the manmade waterfall, as their bodies pulsated to the sounds of the Caribbean music.

Twenty Four

The women began their fantasy three-week vacation by doing everything together, like shopping on Main Street at some of the best diamond and gold shops in the world. Beginning with Cardow's, The Famous Emerald Shop, Little Swiz, and Diamonds in Paradise.

They shopped at the Coach and Fendi outlets, purchased authentic island souvenirs and ate food at The Market Square. They went parasailing, jet skiing, and scuba diving together.

The women ate breakfast at the villa, in between their daily morning massages. Lunch at places like Hook Line and Sinker and dinner at Eunice's.

With an occasional stop at The Chicken Shack, for some of the best fried chicken in St. Thomas.

But the nightlife was the best! From blue light rub-a-dub parties downtown to the Shake What Cha Momma Gave Ya clubs like the Mill. Only later to be chauffeured home and given wonderful late night massages after taking long hot baths in their own private quarters.

"Aaah," Brandy sighed and said, as the men massaged their feet. "Ladies if this is only the end of week one, Sukenya, girl, you may have to postpone your wedding until next year."

"Next year!" squealed Nicole and Alexandria. "Shoot, you may have to postpone your wedding indefinitely because we're never going home!"

The women nodded their heads in agreement and filled the house with laughter as the four men continued to massage and remove every kink and sore spot from their bodies.

After their first fun filled week, the girls decided to spend their second week island hopping and relaxing in the sun. Their first stop was Magens Bay, where they sunbathed and played volleyball with a group visiting from a small town called Cliffwood, New Jersey. Because of Brandy's recent bout with breast cancer, she was the official scorekeeper.

"Hit the ball!" she yelled to Nicole! "Hit the baaaaall. Oops!" she hysterically laughed as she

160

watched her friend fall face first into the sand while trying to spike the ball.

"Will you just keep score?" a sand drenched Nicole yelled over her shoulder to Brandy, while one of the nice gentlemen named Corey attempted to help her up. "Thank you Corey," Nicole laughed as she brushed the sand from her face and hair. "If it weren't for my friend over there," now pointing at Brandy, "we would have won the game."

"Nah," he laughed, "It would have taken more than a missed spiked ball to beat the Johnsons."

"True that," his brother Victor said. "You ladies may be from New Jersey but you haven't played until you've played with the Cliffwood crew."

"Oh please," Sukenya teased, "The only reason why you guys won this time is because we wanted you all to."

"After all," the women chimed in. "We won the first three games!"

They all laughed, shook hands and thanked each other for a fun filled morning.

"Perhaps we'll hook up again before you ladies leave."

"Perhaps," cooed Alexandria. "Because we are going to be here for another week."

"Another week?" The guys excitedly asked.

"Then I know we'll see you lushes ladies again," replied Warren who, had an amazing deep voice that was driving Alexandria crazy.

As the two groups parted, Nicole put her arm around Alexandria and asked between her teeth, "Why Alexandria, must you always flirt?"

"What?" Alexandria wickedly giggled. "I wasn't flirting, I was just having a little harmless fun."

"That's what I'm afraid of my dear cousin," Nicole snickered while shaking her head back and forth. "That's what I'm afraid of."

"But Nikki," Brandy chuckled, "You have to admit, the brothers were definitely eye candy."

"I know that's right," Sukenya interrupted. "Because if that brother Warren would have said Aaah baby to me one mo time..."

The other three women stopped and looked at Sukenya who was unaware that they'd stopped. Sukenya blindly continued walking and talking, as the three women snickered and said in harmony, "Oh no Miss Prim and Proper is not trying to go there!"

Sukenya, now fully aware that the joke was on her simply waved her hand and said, "Forget y'all, I was just going with the flow."

"The flow of what?" Alexandria sarcastically laughed, "Girl, you are getting married in three weeks. The only thing flowing will be you, down the aisle."

The four women cracked up laughing as Alexandria motioned her hand like a wave skipping across the ocean.

"Oh shut up Alex!" Sukenya laughed as the four friends walked arm in arm towards the dock of the Ferry now boarding to go to the beautiful Island of St. John.

The ferry ride lasted about twenty minutes, giving the women a chance to sit back, relax and enjoy the ride. As the ferry docked, to their surprise, they were informed of a major jazz festival going on in town. However, they decided to go directly to the secluded and tranquil Cinnamon Bay Beach also located on the beautiful island, where the white sand and tranquil atmosphere was absolutely breathtaking. From beautiful white wild donkeys strolling calmly along the beach to the sounds of the squirrels and lizards playing hide and seek.

The women laid on the beach for hours listening to the animals playing, the birds singing and the sounds of the waves crashing. Occasionally, they would take a dip in the ocean and sigh, "Aaah, this feels like heaven."

The crystal blue water was so warm and so calm, it shimmered and glistened off of their bodies. The scent of the ocean air allowed the women to inhale their worries and release their burdens. To cleanse their bodies with the best water created by God, ocean seawater, that is. The purest water known to heal bodies from head to toe and to carry all diseases out to sea... Water known as Mother Nature's best medicine. Here is also where the four beautiful women, Nicole, Alexandria, Brandy and Sukenya, all lined in a row, soaked up God's wonderful sun and healed.

"Alex, are you still seeing that man?" Nicole quietly asked.

At first Alexandria pretended not to hear her cousin. After about five minutes Nicole raised her head and looked over at Alexandria.

"No Nicole," Alexandria answered as she stared blankly at the sky. "No I am not." Alexandria paused and said, "You see Nikki I don't need him anymore. Because I now have you Miss Money Bags. Best of all," she grinned, "I don't have to sleep with you!"

The two women chuckled together and continued relaxing.

Brandy pretended not to hear their conversation. She too was aware of Alexandria's indiscretion, but had promised Alex, never to breathe a word to anyone.

As Brandy drifted in and out of consciousness, her mind went back to a conversation she'd had with Alexandria a few months ago...

"Brandy," Alexandria pleaded, "just trust me on this. Believe me when I say, I know what I'm doing! I know in the past, I've done some crazy things. But this time Bran, I'm doing this because I have to! Yes, I love James with all of my heart, but I'm not going to let Triscope get away with hurting my cousin either. I just can't!" she cried. "And yes Brandy, I know Nicole has always been there for me, even when we were children, she was there. So if it means me sleeping with the owner of Triscope for the truth, then God forgive me! Besides, can I help it if the man has a thing for young beautiful blond hair, blue-eyed European women with big breasts? Please trust me on this Brandy," Alexandria pleaded. "Because after I'm finished with him, he will forever know and understand the true meaning of, the wrath of a woman!"

Alexandria turned over on her stomach to allow the sun to tan her back. She looked over at her sleeping and very relaxed cousin and smiled as she quietly said to herself, "for once in my life Nicole, I was able to help you. After all Nikki, it was you who taught me to see and understand why, although my complexion was due to our African, French and Indian heritage, we were both beautiful. It was you Nicole, who at the ripe old age of 8 came to my rescue after I ran home crying because some kids had called me a half-breed and a zebra baby."

Alexandria allowed her mind to return to that painful but very special moment in time.

"Don't cry Alex," Nicole pleaded. *"Let's pray for them because they didn't know any better. Let's pray and ask God to tell their mommies to teach them what our mommies taught us. You remember Alex? Don't you?"* my self-assured eight-year-old cousin asked as she handed me her tissue and said. *"Mommy says on the inside Alex, we are all the same. And that God judges our hearts, and not the color of our skin. And even though, at times people are going to be cruel and insensitive as long as we remember who we are, no one can ever hurt us.*

You remember Alex?" eight year-old Nicole asked again. *"Don't you?"*

"Yes Nicole," Alexandria quietly whispered. Alexandria whispered as if she were answering her childhood memories. "I Remember... I also remember that it was you Nicole who, at 17 convinced me to attend Norfolk State University with you."

"Oh Alex!" Nicole squealed with excitement. "You have to come! It will be a blast!! And just think, we'll be roommates forever!!!" giggled the two teenagers.

Alexandria's eyes filled with tears simply thinking about those days and Nicole's sweet and innocent heart. As she drifted off to sleep, Alexandria smiled peacefully as she allowed her mind to remember all that she had done. It didn't matter to her what anyone else would think, because in her heart she knew, she had done it all in the name of love... *All...* she smiled as she quietly thought out her secret, *in the name of sisterhood.*

167

Twenty Five

After visiting Nicole at St. Mary's Psychiatric Facility, Alexandria strategically set out to find the culprits responsible for sabotaging her cousin. *"She needs rest,"* Alexandria remembered the doctor telling her. *"How long... will she have to stay?"* Alexandria tearfully asked.

"I'm not sure." the doctor replied in a somber but firm voice. *"You see, Nicole is suffering from severe depression, and after her accidental overdose."* It had been no accident. *"It would be best if she remained here for a while..."*

Seeing Nicole in such a horrible state of mind brought out a side of Alexandria that no one ever knew about. Not even Nicole. This was the side of Alexandria who knew nothing but pure hatred. The side that remained buried deep inside the smallest corner of her heart and mind. This was the side of Alexandria, who as a child growing up in a predominately black neighborhood, never forgave or forgot the cruelty of other children. She however, had taught herself how to control that evil person inside of her and to never let her surface. But, Alexandria never forgot she was there.

Had it not been for Nicole's purest love for her cousin, Alexandria would have surely become not only cynical but also very deadly!
When Alexandria walked out of St. Mary's that day, there was only one thought on her mind. Revenge!

"If vengeance is mine sayeth the Lord, then God," she screamed, "I sure hope you're with me because as of this very moment, I...am... revenge!"

It took Alexandria three months of intense detective work to find out who was responsible for Nicole's misfortune. Alexandria started at the bottom, *the place where you can always find answers,* she'd often say. Besides, Nicole always said the maintenance and the cleaning staff were her best friends, friends who never once believed she was guilty.

Nicole's loyal friends allowed Alexandria to impersonate one of the nightly cleaning staff, thereby giving her free reign to the entire building. Including the office of current CEO Mr. Tom Jackovich.

Because of Tom's quirkiness, she knew he was not the mastermind behind Nicole's setup.

She remembered Nicole often saying, *"It is as if Tom is untouchable, as if there is someone of a higher authority allowing him to get away with his reign of terror."*

Alexandria spent many hours going over Tom's files. She had learned how to pick locks by purchasing a *'how to'* video off of the internet and mastered the technique prior to going into Tom's office and neatly rummaging through his files. Surprisingly nothing ever seemed out of the ordinary. However, one night Alexandria noticed the name Sam Burgess on several files with Nicole's name on them. While the files looked normal, Sam's name always seemed to appear very small and always in the lower right hand corner of his files. *Who is Sam Burgess?* she wondered. "Nicole never mentioned his name before," she said out loud.

Alexandria later questioned a few employees and found out that Mr. Sam Burgess was none other than the current owner of Triscope, a company he'd inherited from the original and now deceased owner, Mr. Fred Hines, Sam's one and only brother in law!

Sam was also the man who had hand picked and hired Mr. Tom Jackovich to be his new CEO.

Mr. Sam Burgess, a man whose main office was on the other side of town away from Triscope.

Bingo, Alexandria silently smiled.

Once Alexandria found out the culprit was none other than the original owner, Fred Hines's brother-in-law, Mr. Sam Burgess, her wrath began. "My poor sweet naive cousin," Alexandria sighed. "If only you knew Nikki," she whispered while slowly shaking her head back and forth. "If only you knew."

For the next three months, Alexandria studied Sam's every movement. She found out his likes and his dislikes. His must haves, and should not haves. Which included the dark side of his must haves and secrets from his past. A past that would certainly cause his very wealthy wife and sole heir of the infamous Hines Empire to not only divorce him, but leave him destitute as well.

Alexandria began her wrath by first withdrawing all of the money she had inherited many years ago from her parent's accidental death settlement. She then convinced Sam's private secretary of many years into retiring early.

"Who needs a 401-K?" Sam's secretary laughed, "When someone makes you an offer like this."

However, before her sudden departure, she recommended Sam interview her very young, beautiful and voluptuous niece.

"I never knew you had a niece," he said.

"There's a lot you don't know about me," she laughed as she said her goodbyes and moved to the Cayman Islands.

Three days later...

Alexandria walked into the interview wearing a short, tight, navy blue Ann Taylor suit. Showing enough cleavage to make the 69 year-old Mr. Burgess blush with embarrassment.

Damn, he thought to himself while licking his lips. *This is a dream come true,* he silently squealed. *A dream come true.*

The beautiful and shapely 5'11", blond haired, blue-eyed bombshell was hired without so much as taking a typing test. What Mr. Burgess didn't realize was that this was the beginning to his end.

One month later...

"Thank you, Thank you, Thank you," he yelled as he rode Alexandria, so he thought, like he was about to win the Kentucky Derby! "Aaah!" he screamed as he fell on top of her. But then, there was silence. A dreaded silence that no woman ever wants to hear, especially if you've just finished sexing up a 69 year old.

"*Oh shit!*" she thought to herself. "*Oh shit! Oh shit! Please don't let this man be dead. Please don't let this man be!...*" she yelled as she rolled him off of her, "...dead..."

He wasn't dead. Not in the least. This fool was actually smiling and crying at the same time.

"Thaaaaaat was ammmazing," he finally said. "I never imagined these Viagra pills would work like this!"

You call that working, Alexandria laughed to herself. *Geeze, I could have had a V8!*

For the next two years, Alexandria gave Sam the best sex he'd ever known. She held nothing back, and left nothing to his imagination. He truly believed he had found a goddess. Many times, after their intense sessions, Alexandria would profess her undying love to him by saying their age difference didn't matter.

"I just want to love you," she'd say. "Sam, I want to know all your thoughts, your secrets and your desires, anything you tell me will be held right here in my heart." Which just happened to be right in between her size 38 DD's.

Once Alexandria had Sam *"whipped,"* she knew it would only be a matter of time before he started telling her everything she needed to know. After about a year, Sam began confiding in Alexandria. He told her all about how he and his directors had set up this uppity black bitch who he felt, had forgotten her place. He laughed as he described in detail how he had hired a man who was notorious for getting rid of militants in large companies. He continued laughing as he told her how they had set up this woman named Nicole and had humiliated her by not only having her arrested at her office but by also having the detectives walk her out in handcuffs down a long corridor right in front of everyone And how he had paid off the woman's husband to not only leave her at the most critical time in her life, but to divorce her as well.

"I made her an example to her peers," he said. "And a reminder to those who may have ever considered selling me out."

Sam then began to laugh. The sound of him laughing sent chills up and down Alexandria's spine, and made her blood boil. But the person that she held deep inside her inner mind and heart allowed her to laugh as well.

Then one night, after an unforgettable evening of sex, Alexandria never allowed herself to think of it as making love, Sam gave Alexandria the silver bullet she knew would finally bring him down. Sam told Alexandria how he had been responsible for his own brother-in-law's, Mr. Fred Hines's, death!

He told Alexandria how Fred was his wife Helen's only brother. And how they were from what was once considered a blue blood line of money, that is, money that came from a long heritage of wealth.

Their astronomical total fortune made someone like Bill Gates' fortune look like chump change.

Sam, who came from nothing, admitted how he had only married Helen for her money. And how he hated the fact that their wealth meant nothing to them. Sam also resented Fred for his very down to earth mannerism and would often ask, "Why Fred, would someone with all of your power and money want to work elbow to elbow with the common folks? "This is our company," Sam laughed, now mocking the deceased Fred. "A family company, a company where, we are all equal. Yadda, yadda, yadda," Sam laughed as he remembered Fred's answer.

"Oh give me a break!" he told Fred, "If I ran this company, I would be in charge and that's it. The employees would be the least of my worries," he squawked. "Their job would be to come here and work for me not with me."

"That, my dear brother-in-law," a stunned Fred replied, "is why you will never run Triscope!"

However, the more Sam thought about the company the better he liked his idea.

Within months of that conversation, Sam put out a contract on Fred by using a 99.9 percent accurate method, a tragic and unexplainable plane crash.

"It's a pity," he told Alexandria. "That other passengers had to die. If only Nicole, Fred's confidante and protégé had been on that flight as originally scheduled, we wouldn't be battling this long ass trial now," he snarled. "Once I realized Nicole wasn't on the now doomed flight, I knew it would take a heavy-hitter to help me bring her down, which is how Tom and Sheila became involved. Tom followed my instructions to a 'T.' And so did Sheila. Sheila however was simply a weak pawn in my game.

In an effort to tie up any loose ends. Upon her release from prison, I had her run down in broad daylight. Can you believe it Alexandria?" he asked. "Sheila actually thought upon her release from prison, I was going to give her $3 million."

Sam paused for a moment as he thought about Sheila and said, "Not."

He began to laugh, and laugh and laugh. As usual, the sound of Sam's loud and obnoxious laugh sent chills up and down Alexandria's spine and made her blood boil. Alexandria, however, laughed as well. At times, she laughed harder than Sam.

That night, Alexandria went home and took her normal scalding hot shower, something she always did after an evening with Sam. This particular night, Alexandria cried longer and harder than usual. Just thinking about how that bastard had killed Fred, Sheila and damn near came so close to taking Nicole's life, brought the person from that small inner place within her heart and mind, all the way out! But Alexandria remembered to thank God for sparing her cousin, by sending Nicole and her then husband Brian to Jamaica during that horrible time. "Speaking of Brian," she hissed. "One day "B." But not right now."

During Nicole's final week in court, Alexandria contacted Chris and told him of her two-year tryst with Mr. Sam Burgess. She told Chris how, fortunate for her, Sam had always allowed her to pick the places for them to meet for their rendezvous. For this reason, Alexandria had managed to not only record every conversation and unmentionable act they had performed, but she had also video taped them as well!

At first, Chris reprimanded Alexandria saying, "Alexandria! You can't just go around taping people without their knowledge. That's illegal."

"Don't you think I know that?" Alexandria sarcastically replied. "What he did to Nicole is illegal too. And don't forget about poor Fred, Sheila and all those passengers on that doomed plane."

"OK Alexandria," Chris quickly replied. "Let me see what I can do. Can you give me a couple of days?" he anxiously asked.

"Sure Chris," Alexandria answered in a far away and distant voice. "I'll give you your time. But I'm warning you Chris... Before I let Sam and Tom get off Scott free, oh,oh,oh!" she growled, "on that final day," she paused. "When they think they have won." She paused again and screamed, "I will calmly walk into that courtroom, and blow both their fucking heads off! Do I make myself clear Chris?" she snarled.

Chris had never heard Alexandria use that tone before. She seemed different, almost eerie. What frightened him even more, Chris knew from the sound of Alexandria's voice, she was serious.

After two days of thinking, Chris devised a plan that would have to run like clockwork.

He knew that because Alexandria had never come to any of Nicole's courtroom sessions, no one in

178

the room knew what she looked like. Chris therefore was going to call her as a surprise character witness. He told Alexandria to wear her hair natural and to pray that Mr. Burgess would see the resemblance and realize that he'd been had. What Chris never anticipated was Alexandria showing up late.

After Nicole's grueling cross-examination, Chris was furious as he paced back and forth, asking himself over and over again, "Where in the hell is Alexandria?"

Which is whom Nicole saw Chris trying to reach on his cell phone during their ten-minute recess.

"Alexandria you knew the plan!" he mumbled over and over again, as he paced back and forth. "She knew how important it was for her to be here today. After all, This is Nicole's final day!" Suddenly, Chris had a horrible sick feeling in the pit of his stomach as he remembered Alexandria's threat!

"Oh man." He quietly said out loud, "I sure hope Alexandria is not waiting out there for the right moment to come in here and start blasting this place like the women from the movie 'Set It Off!' Oh man!" he sighed with a feeling of unbelievable fear. By now, Chris's mind was racing in all directions and his heart was beating faster than ever, as the judge banged his gavel and said, "Court is now in sess."

Chris saw from the corner of his eye the courtroom doors fly open. As he turned and focused, he observed Alexandria entering the courtroom and walking quickly towards the front. It was then at that precise moment, Chris later told Alexandria, that because of her earlier threat, he didn't know whether to grab Nicole and yell "take cover," or what!

***

When Alexandria walked into the courtroom that day, and whispered to Nicole, Sam instantly knew he'd been had. He decided, right then and there, that he would rather confess to a discrimination lawsuit and pay out a huge lump sum of money than face the embarrassment of the public obtaining knowledge of him having an affair with a woman young enough to be his granddaughter. Not to mention the possibility of facing not one, not two, but several murder charges.

"*Damn,*" he thought to himself. "*She knows everything! If my wife ever found out that I was responsible for murdering her baby brother, she'd make damn sure I died a penniless old man in some horrible nursing home or worse yet, prison! At 72 years old, I'm not going back to that way of life for anyone!*

180

I know what I'll do. I'll plead guilty to all of Nicole's charges. Then," he paused and mumbled, *"I'll* offer Nicole an out of court settlement for $1 Billion dollars! Shit! 1 billion is peanuts compared to what Helen has!" *"Besides," he silently laughed, "at least I will still have my company!"*

"Your Honor!" he yelled. "I would like to confess!"

***

"When I walked into the courtroom that day," Alexandria smiled, "Sam knew he'd been had. What he didn't know then was that Nicole and I were first cousins. What he didn't know then was that for almost two years, he'd been sleeping with a proud African American woman.

But oh if I could have been a fly on the wall, and seen his face when he received that special package in the mail explaining every sordid detail. Showing all of his dried up glory, and listening to him confess all of his sins.

Oh, if I were a fly on the wall watching him react to my information. I probably would have fallen off the wall and died from laughing. For my final act, I included a beautifully written note that said," *In the event of my untimely death or anyone closely related to me, copies of this videotape will be distributed to several newsrooms throughout the country. Pray, old man that I live forever!*

Signed by no other than ... Me.

Alexandria imagined Sam reading the note and laughed as she finally drifted off to sleep and allowed the sounds of the crashing waves to carry her secret out to sea.

Twenty Six

Two hours later...

"Okay girls," a beautifully tanned Sukenya announced. "I think we've had enough sun. Let's go into town and attend the jazz festival."

The other women agreed, took a final dip in the ocean and proceeded towards the sounds of the live bands.

Once in town, they decided to take in the live jazz sounds by sitting on the outside of one of the many restaurants that surrounded the bands while they enjoyed the tropical breeze and sipped on Island Punch.

"This is sooo awesome!" Sukenya squealed. "How are we ever going to go home after all of this? And just think," she continued. "In three weeks, we'll all be dancing at my wed..."

Sukenya paused midstream of her sentence and squinted her eyes at a figure she noticed playing on stage. As her eyes focused, she couldn't believe what she saw. Sukenya placed her hands over her mouth in utter disbelief and let out a slight gasp! To be certain, she got up from her seat, and slowly began to walk towards the stage. As she moved closer, her eyes began to fill with tears. Because... there dressed in all white holding an exquisitely polished gold saxophone caressing it ever so gently, was none other than Sukenya's long lost love, Mr. Austin Kincaid, playing in the band, looking better than she could have ever imagined.

Austin Kincaid was a renowned saxophone player who had performed with some of the most famous musicians in the business. And now, here after nine years and many tears without so much as a phone call, standing less than three feet away from Sukenya was the man who at one time she loved and cherished more than life itself, doing what he loved and desired more than her... playing his saxophone.

Sukenya and Austin were childhood friends, teenage sweethearts and young adult lovers.

"He is the one and only man I will ever truly love," she once confided in Brandy.

What seemed to be a lifetime romance, ended suddenly when Austin chose his musical career over Sukenya and moved to California. His leaving broke Sukenya's heart into a million unbearable pieces. In an effort to minimize her pain, Sukenya vowed never to allow herself to love anyone that deeply again.

That was before she met Greg. And now exactly three weeks before her wedding, here stands Austin.

As Austin focused on Sukenya, he gave her a wink and a warm smile, something he often did when they were together so many years ago. Luckily for them, his session was ending just as Sukenya walked up.

Austin quickly said, "Hello Boo." A pet name he'd given her while she was in college.

"Austin!" Sukenya squealed with excitement. "What are you doing here?"

"I'm working," he laughed. "Nah, seriously. I'm here this week performing in the St. John's Jazz Festival. God girl you look great!" He smiled as he grabbed her hand. "Turn around so I can see you," he teased as he slowly turned Sukenya around in a circle while he observed all of her fine features. Then said in a low husky voice, "yeah, you still got it. I mean, damn Boo, you are still as fine as ever!"

"*He always did know how to compliment me,*" she thought to herself. "Well you're not looking half bad yourself Austin," she replied while still holding his hand.

As Sukenya and Austin became reacquainted, Brandy, Alexandria and Nicole walked up on the two old friends.

"Well," Alexandria growled in a semi sarcastic voice. "Look what rose out of the ashes!"

"Good to see you too," Austin replied. "Still a smart ass I see." He laughed as the two embraced.

"Talk about a twist of fate!" Nicole interrupted.

"Hey Nikki." Austin smiled. "It's been a long time."

"Not long enough," Nicole mumbled under her breath, then replied, "Yes Austin, a lot has happened since we last saw you."

"I know Miss Billionaire!" he joked as the two embraced. "Good news travels fast!"

"Well then," Brandy interrupted in a not so friendly tone, "I guess you've also heard..." She smiled and looked directly at Sukenya. "...Sukenya is getting married in three weeks."

Brandy was still angry with Austin for leaving and breaking her best friend's heart, and she wasn't about to try and hide her feelings.

"Married!" a surprised Austin repeated as he turned and looked at Sukenya with wide eyes, who, at that same moment, shot Brandy an icy and annoyed look.

"Yes Austin," she halfheartedly answered. "Three weeks from today, I'll be Mrs. Gregory Hollingsworth III."

"Damn!" he replied as he grabbed her left hand. "From the size of this rock on your finger, the brother is clocking some serious dollars. Congratulations Sukenya," he smiled. "I'm really happy for you baby. Let me be the first to kiss the bride."

With that, Austin slowly pulled Sukenya into his arms and kissed her in a way she never imagined. Nor did she expect the feelings she thought she had buried so deep inside her soul so many years ago, to come flooding back as if it were yesterday. But here they were, back and stronger than ever.

It was as if Sukenya had stepped back into time.

Brandy on the other hand, sucked her teeth in total disgust, and looked away.

Twenty Seven

For the next week and a half, Austin and Sukenya were inseparable. They enjoyed horseback riding and swimming at Trunk Bay. They went dancing at all the major hot spots in town and went parasailing, jet skiing and snorkeling at Coki Beach. They toured museums and went on submarine rides, and even shared a beautiful private lunch in tranquil Tortola.

No matter how they spent their days, they spent every evening taking long moonlit walks on various beaches throughout St. Thomas.

It was there, on Sapphire Beach, where Austin confessed to Sukenya his inability to get over her. According to Austin, Sukenya was his one and only true love and soul mate.

"I know I hurt you Sukenya when I left for California," he said. "But in my heart, I always believed that one day, we would be together again. And yes I know that I also promised to send for you once I got settled, but in this business Sukenya, everything moves so fast. One day turned into one week, one week turned into three months and here we are nine years later. Believe me when I say, I don't know where the time went.

What I do know Sukenya is ... I love you. I always have, and I always will. Sukenya baby, you were born to be my wife," he whispered. "My wife and no one else's. I know I don't have the right to say any of this, but I have to know where we stand before you leave tomorrow...

Just think about it Sukenya, for the past week and a half we've spent all of our time together. Surely you don't think it is a coincidence that we ended up on an Island together after all of these years do you? I believe we were destined to be together. I feel it in my heart and I think you feel it too. But you're too afraid to surrender and to give into your feelings. Sukenya baby," he pleaded. "You were never afraid of me before, please don't be afraid of me now. Because I'm here Sukenya. I'm here," he whispered as he held her ever so close. "In this time... In this place... On this island. Our island, and I'm never leaving you again."

Austin allowed his words to make love to Sukenya's mind. He played on her every emotion. She was drunk from words and dizzy with confusion.

"How can I deny what is standing right in front of me?" she asked herself. *"How can I deny myself the one man whom for past nine years I've longed and ached for? And why should I? After all, tonight is only the beginning right? This is who I truly belong with right? It couldn't be a coincidence that we ended up on the same island together... Could it? Not after all these years..."*

"I love you Austin" were the only words Sukenya allowed Austin to hear.

How noble of Austin to tell Sukenya his true feelings on the eve of her departure back to New Jersey.

Austin and Sukenya retired to her private master quarters with precise instructions not to be disturbed. For Sukenya truly believed she had been given a second chance with her first love.

Austin had made his pleas sound, so honest, so enticing and so genuine. After all, Austin's words were the words Sukenya had waited so many years to hear. Nine years to be exact. Nine years and many tears, had she forgotten?

"I'm not going to blow it this time," Sukenya confided in Brandy earlier that evening. "I know you don't understand, but please accept my decision!" she pleaded.

Now as the two soul mates sipped wine in front of her marble fireplace and listened to *Gill Scott's* CD, they talked about old times as well as new times. As the evening progressed, Austin and Sukenya continued their night of passion. When what began as a chance meeting a week and a half ago combined with smoldering desires once securely locked away for the past nine years patiently simmering, abruptly ignited into what was now a full five-alarm fire! Their volcanic desires were to say the least, oozing like hot lava.

As Sukenya began to unlock what for so long had held her hostage, she anxiously asked Austin.

"What am I going to tell Greg?"

Austin looked up at Sukenya and replied in a raspy voice, "The truth."

"Which is? ..." Sukenya curiously asked, now clearly interrupting his flow.

Austin paused, looked at Sukenya, and smiled as he placed his hands on each side of her face and gently pulled her towards him and replied, "The truth my love... is... you and I belong together... We always

191

have and we always will. You my dear sweet Sukenya, are my soul mate... My never ending circle of life!"

Austin's words were the only words Sukenya needed to hear. His words made Sukenya forever want to be a part of his past and all of his present. His words were smooth and seductive. As smooth as if he were playing his saxophone. But then, Austin said something that brought Sukenya back into reality.

"After you get home Sukenya, break off your wedding with Greg and wait for me. I'm scheduled to start a world tour next week in Japan. The tour is going to last a year and a half. Once the tour ends, I'll fly to New Jersey, where we'll get married and move to California."

They had gotten sooo close to the fire. So very, very close. So close, but no cigar.

"Excuse me Austin?" a somewhat surprised Sukenya asked as she stood up. "Let me get this straight. You want me... to..." she paused and placed her hands on her hips, "break off my wedding with Greg, then wait a year and a half for you, while you trail across the world, and then get married? Not to mention that last part about me giving up all that I have accomplished and moving out to California! Oh hell no!" she screamed as she said, "You self-centered bastard! What in the hell do you take me for?"

Sukenya placed her hand on her head and said, "Now I remember what happened nine years ago! Now I remember! It's like the same old shit all over again!" Sukenya screamed. "Austin, you said those same words to me nine years ago, just before you left me standing at the fucking airport! Don't you remember Austin?" she yelled.

"Shhh. Baby," he replied. "Why are you getting so excited?"

"Excited!" Sukenya laughed in a high-pitched wicked voice. "I'm not excited Austin. I'm remembering! I'm remembering you saying," now mocking Austin's voice, *Wait for me Sukenya. After I get settled in California, I'll send for you.* Remember that Austin?" she screamed! "Don't you remember Austin? Please! Don't play me stupid Austin because I know you remember!

After all Austin, those were your precise words to me nine years ago," a stunned and angry Sukenya said as she paced back and forth in front of Austin with her hands on her hips and her eyes blazing.

But amazingly for the first time in nine years, as Sukenya exhaled Austin, she breathed in new life.

"The first year Austin, I waited patiently for you to settle in. I guess you never settled in, did you Austin?" she screamed. "Did you? The next two years, I walked around like a zombie because I missed you so much. I cried daily Austin, because of the constant stabbing pain I felt in my heart.

Because of that pain, I vowed never ever to allow anyone to hurt me like that again. I vowed never to love anyone that deeply again. And why Austin?" she screamed. "All behind you and your sorry ass bottomless promises! Did you really think after nine years of nothing, you could simply sweet talk me into giving up all that I have worked for?" she asked. "Did you?"

"I," she paused and pointed at herself. "Am one of the top news anchorwomen in the country! Not to mention," she screamed as tears began to swell up in her eyes like a swollen river about to crest, "have a real man at home who genuinely loves and respects me for who I am. And," she screamed, "places me first in his life. Not after some world fucking tour. Not after a major gig here or a major gig there! And especially not after all of the major holidays!"

Sukenya's tears spilled over, as she remembered her past relationship with Austin as well as her current relationship with Greg.

Austin finally responded to Sukenya's triumphant testimony by saying, "But Sukenya, I love you."

"What!" Sukenya hissed. "Oh sure Austin you may think you love me. Hell, I don't even think you know if that's true! What I do know," now walking towards her bedroom door. "Is, that you do not and cannot eeever love me the way in which I need and want to be loved. And, I thank you soooo very much Mr. Austin Kincaid for helping me finally realize all that I was about to throw away. Now get the fuck out!" Sukenya yelled as she flung the double doors of her private suite open.

As the doors flew open, to their surprise, there stood Brandy, Nicole and Alexandria. Austin grabbed his jacket and softly walked past the four women without uttering a single word. As he walked towards the door to leave, KiKi and Ty shooed him out of their house.

That night the women spent their final stay in beautiful St. Thomas drinking several bottles of wine and consoling Sukenya.

A short time after Austin had left, Alexandria looked up at Sukenya and said, "Hey Suk, I just thought about something. In all my years of knowing you," she laughed. "I haaave never eeever heard you use the 'F' word before. You go girl!"

The four friends cracked up laughing, they laughed right up until it was time to leave.

After three amazing weeks, it was now time to go home. The plane ride home was relatively quiet. Brandy missed her husband and her children. Alexandria missed James. Sukenya not only missed Greg, but for the first time in her life, she felt free... mind, body and soul.

Nicole missed her company and was eager to see how Chris had managed her business during her absence. Her vacation had given her a great deal of justice, just as Chris had suggested. She was now mentally and physically stronger than ever before. She was as vibrant as the day she walked across the podium at Norfolk State University some 15 years ago. Only now, because of life's wonderful lessons, Nicole was truly a much wiser and grounded woman. She was, in all instances, whole again!

As the women arrived at Newark Airport, they were greeted with welcome home hugs, kisses, flowers and balloons. After three glorious weeks away from their significant others, you know the brothers were as horny as hell. Needless to say, no one got much sleep that night.

Twenty Eight

Today is Monday, Nicole's first day back to work. After three wonderful weeks of vacation it was now time to get back to business.

"Whew," she sighed as she drove into the parking lot of her consulting firm. "In five days, Sukenya will be marrying the right man. All of her preparations have been taken care of and Sukenya has nothing to do now except relax and wait."

To Nicole's surprise, there was a long stretch black Lexus limo sitting in her private parking space. *Whose Limo is this?* she asked herself. *And why is it parked in my parking space? I spoke with Chris several times this weekend, and he never mentioned anything to me about a new client.* "Oh well," she said out loud. "No biggie. Perhaps it's a wealthy client," she laughed as she pulled into the parking spot next to the limo.

Nicole stepped out of her car, walked around and observed the limo as she said, "Sure is a nice car."

Suddenly, Nicole froze in absolute terror as she noticed the personalized license plate on the limo which read...OWNR – Triscope!

At first Nicole thought she had misread the personalized plates but then realized she hadn't.

"Oh God!" she said out loud as she grabbed her chest in an attempt to try and calm her pounding heart.

Nicole immediately thought of Chris and pulled out her Motorola cell phone to call him. As his phone rang, Nicole paced back and forth in front of the limo, staring at the license plate. She was too afraid to do anything else.

"Hi this is Chris, I can't come to the phone right now..."

"Damn!" she said out loud, "I hate voicemails!" But then quickly said, "Chris, hi this is Nicole. When you get this message, please call me back ASAP! It's an emergency!"

Nicole hung up her phone and began to lightly tap her forehead.

"Okay Nikki girl," she said out loud, "don't panic. Just take ten deep breaths and focus. Breathe in and out. In...One...And out... In...Two... and out." Nicole breathed and counseled with herself as she remembered what her therapist, the fine doctor had once told her.

"Nicole when you feel a panic attack coming on, try and focus on something amusing. Then take ten deeep soul cleansing breaths. Just breathe and focus," he would say, "breathe and focus." Nicole was breathing, but the only object she could focus on was the license plate on the limo. And that sure as hell wasn't amusing.

What would my fine doctor say now? she thought.

As Nicole began to regain her composure, she suddenly asked herself out loud, "Hey wait a minute, what am I afraid of?" Nicole quickly gathered up her belongings and boldly walked through the front doors of her computer consulting firm.

"Welcome back Nicole!" squealed her employees. "You look great!" they all said in harmony.

"St. Thomas is just what you needed," her personal assistant, Ashley smiled as she gave Nicole an affectionate hug. "You look sooo fabulous and well-rested girl."

"Thank you Ashley." Nicole smiled. "And uhh Ashley, thank you for agreeing to work for me after that horrible fiasco at Triscope. Thank you for believing in me," Nicole said in a warm and humble voice.

"Always Boss Lady," Ashley laughed. "Always... But I think you better get to your office," she quickly said, "because Chris has been in there for about an hour!"

"Chris is here?" a puzzled Nicole asked.

"Yuper," Ashley replied. "He's in there with someone who he says is an old friend of yours."

"An old friend of mine?" Nicole asked.

She was now totally confused.

As Nicole walked into her office, there was Chris. He was sitting behind her desk with a huge grin on his face.

"Well welcome back stranger," he laughed as he stood up and walked towards her. "You must think you're still on vacation." He chuckled as he gave her a warm and comforting hug and said, "We've been waiting for you for over an hour."

"We?" Nicole asked as she looked into Chris's eyes searching for an answer.

"Yes," replied a strange but familiar sounding voice. "We... but tell me this, why is it, whenever I come to the United States, I have to wait for hours just to see you?" laughed the strange but familiar voice.

Nicole attempted to see where the voice was coming from by trying to look over Chris's shoulder. But because of Chris's height, she saw nothing.

Chris then stepped out of Nicole's way, and allowed her to focus on whom the strange but familiar sounding voice belonged to.

"Oh my God!" Nicole screamed with excitement as her eyes filled with tears. "Oh my God! Sanjay!" she screamed. "Is that really you? Oh my God!" she cried as she walked over and gave him the biggest hug. "I can't believe this! When did you get here?" she asked. "How long are you staying?"

Nicole was now clearly emotional and very happy to see the former owner of Sintech.

"I arrived last night," he laughed. "And am on my way to the airport as we speak."

"You're leaving so soon?" she asked in a disappointing voice.

"Yes, I have much business to take care of back home," he replied. "But don't worry, I'll be here when ever you need me."

"But there is so much I wanted to tell you," she said. "I mean Sanjay, Sintech was your baby."

"As," interrupted Sanjay, "Triscope *is* your pride and joy."

"But so much has happened since then." Nicole sighed.

"Yes I know," Sanjay said in a comforting fatherly tone. "You do not know this Nicole," he said as he motioned her to sit with him on *her* sofa. "But I visited you while you were at St. Mary's."

"You did?" she asked.

"Yes child," he affectionately replied, "and it broke my heart to see someone with such great potential, innocence and beauty in such a horrible state. I sought after and found the best doctors through out the world to come here to the United States and help you regain your power. Luckily, the best doctors were already here. As time went on and I saw you getting stronger, I hired Chris to be your attorney, confidante and friend. Think about it," he laughed. "In the entire time that you've known Chris, have you ever seen him with another client?"

"Now that you mention it," Nicole laughed, as she looked up at Chris, "No... No I haven't."

"That's because," Sanjay smiled, "he is yours exclusively! You see Nicole, Chris is my nephew, however, he has been here in the United States all of his life. How ironic that I asked him to look out for someone so close to his own age. Just look at you Nicole." he smiled. "You're beautiful and you're back! Stronger and even more confident than the young woman who trailed across the country to the Middle East and beat out every bidder for Sintech, with nothing more than her charm and honesty. Only later to be tricked by your own employer upon your return home, and never once given the proper respect that you so deserved. Perhaps one day," he continued, "the world will finally realize, we are all God's children and if we all work together as he so wants, we will all prosper. With that said young lady, I have a gift for you."

Sanjay opened up his briefcase and pulled out an envelope and handed it to Nicole. Nicole slowly opened the envelope, and noticed a deed. As Nicole read the words on the contract, she blinked her eyes several times, trying to make sure her eyes saw and understood what her brain was reading. The two finally agreed and allowed her voice to read the deed aloud. As Nicole opened her mouth, the words, *"Nicole Jones, Exclusive Owner of Triscope Computer Corporations,"* came out.

Sanjay cleared his throat and said, "I think Mr. Hines would have wanted it this way Nicole. Don't you?" he asked. "I told you many years ago Nicole that one day, our paths would cross again, and now they have. Although," he smiled as he hugged the utterly speechless and shocked woman, "I'm sure we will see each other again."

Sanjay then turned and shook his nephew's hand, and said, "Chris, always take care of her because she is truly of a rare quality. Just as you are my dear nephew," laughed the very wealthy sheik. "Just as you are. But from the looks of things I can tell you two already know that." he smiled as he said, "Good-bye to you both."

As Sanjay walked towards the door he quickly turned around and said, "Oh, Nicole, I almost forgot. I hope you enjoy your new Lexus Limo! That's a personal gift from me."

Mr. Sanjay left as suddenly as he had arrived.

So, In addition to the one billion-dollar settlement, Nicole was now the sole owner of Triscope Corporations.

Twenty Nine

Today is Tuesday, Sukenya's wedding is now four days away and all of her arrangements have been taken care of.

"There's only one thing left to do," Brandy squealed with excitement during her three-way phone conversation.

"So ladies, are you thinking what I'm thinking?" Nicole laughed.

"Well of course we are," Alexandria chuckled. "But you both know Ms. Prim and proper wants no part of it."

Sukenya's friends knew she was not keen on the idea of a traditional bachelorette party, as they laughed and remembered a conversation they had had with her concerning one a while back.

"I *really don't understand it,*" Sukenya said. "What is so exciting about some half-naked strange man dancing all around you? Especially just before your wedding. I mean like, what's the point?"

"That's the answer!" Alexandria snickered. "To get the point!"

"Oh stop it Alex!" The women laughed as they teased Sukenya about her question.

In lieu of that conversation, the women decided to give Sukenya a surprise bachelorette party she'd never forget.

"Oh it will be fun," Nicole laughed, as the three-way phone conversation continued. "We will have it at my house on Thursday night. This way, she can spend all day Friday being pampered before her big day!"

Greg's friends, on the other hand, decided to throw his bachelor party on the traditional Friday night before his wedding...

As Thursday morning rolled around, the women spent their entire day preparing for Sukenya's surprise, bachelorette party. They were pulling out all of the stops for Sukenya's evening of fun. Nicole hired a caterer to strategically place various trays of exotic hors d'oeuvres in two sections of her gorgeous home, which she stylishly decorated with 100 of the most beautiful scented candles ever imagined. The scented fragrances supplied the house with a warm aroma of vanilla, strawberries, jasmine and mango. Chilled champagne flowed freely from the frozen beaks of two ice-sculptured doves set up in Nicole's great room.

As the guest's arrived, they were each greeted with a glass of chilled champagne and given a ticket to hold on to. Each ticket held a special message for Sukenya who arrived at her party promptly at 7:30 and was greeted with the infamous word 'surprise!' Although she wasn't really surprised, she put on a great act.

"How can you surprise someone two days before their wedding?" Sukenya laughed as she greeted her guests. "Tonight is simply a celebration about new beginnings and an evening of fun."

As the evening of fun began, the ladies laughed, opened gifts and read cards from well-wishers.

"Sukenya, may your life be filled with all the success and happiness you so deserve."

"Good luck Sukenya, we love you."

"Girl it's about time!"

Later that evening, the women decided to play a game from their past. A game called Twister!

"Twister!" everyone yelled.

"Yes ya old farts," Alexandria laughed. "Twister."

"Girl, I can't bend!" yelled Asia. "You know I have bad knees," she laughed as she leaned over in her chair and began rubbing her knees while shouting, "Oh my knees girl. My knees."

"Oh don't be silly," Alexandria jokingly mocked. "Who said anything about bending? This is Twister Alexandria style."

"That figures," Asia laughed in a dry sounding voice.

"Ladies do you all have your tickets?" Alexandria asked.

"Let's begin!" the women cheerfully yelled in excitement.

Alexandria spun the wheel and yelled, "Right foot blue!"

"Who has a blue ticket?" Nicole asked.

"I do, I do," yelled one woman.

The woman walked over to Sukenya and read her ticket which said, "Something old, something new, something borrowed and something blue!" With that, she handed Sukenya a beautiful oblong shaped blue suede box. The box had a small note attached to it, which simply read, *all my love, Greg.* Sukenya's eyes became a little misty as she opened the box and observed a blue sapphire and diamond princess cut necklace. The necklace matched Sukenya's four-carat princess cut blue sapphire and diamond engagement ring given to her by Greg, when he proposed.

"Left foot Green!"

The woman with the green ticket walked over and said as she handed Sukenya a green wallet. "Green represents honor. Tonight, Sukenya we're here to honor you." Sukenya slowly opened the wallet and observed one hundred $100 bills!

"Right foot Red!"

Alexandria, Brandy and Nicole stood up together and read in unison, "Roses are red, violets are blue may you always know just how much we love you!" Together, the three women handed Sukenya a beautiful white heart shaped pearl beaded box.

As Sukenya opened the box, she let out a slight gasp and looked up at her three smiling friends who simply said, "May these three-carat princess cut diamond earrings always remind you of your three sisters."

"That's a carat a piece Sukenya," Alexandria teased.

Sukenya was now truly surprised.

The final part of the evening consisted of the women learning the latest dance called *The Cha-Cha.*

Or as some simply call it, The New Electric Slide. Some of the women bumped into each other, stepped on one another's toes and laughed uncontrollably when asked, "How low can you go?"

Just when the women thought they had mastered the dance, in walked four of the most gorgeous men Nicole's guests had ever laid their eyes on. Instantly, the women started screaming and howling with laughter as the men showed them a few moves to the dance they unknowingly missed.

"Jump ladies! One time, two times, cha-cha, now freeze," a delighted KiKi ordered.

"Hey Asia, what happened to your knees?" Alexandria teased.

Everyone in the room roared with laughter. Sukenya laughed hysterically as she watched her four island friends give the women a show they'd never forget. After all, these were not strange men who were dancing and performing for her unsuspecting friends. They were her four island friends whose hands had been all over her body many times before while in beautiful St. Thomas.

Nicole, Alexandria and Brandy gave each other high fives as they observed their friend having the time of her life.

After all of the guests had gone, Sukenya gave KiKi, Ty, Jason and Bobby a huge hug as she thanked them and the girls for making this "the best surprise ever."

"No need to thank us," laughed KiKi. "Cause gurl," he grinned. "We are here to beat that face and body of yours into per-fec-tion!"

"That's right," Ty agreed. "And you know the hair is mine," he laughed. "Ewe," he squealed as he turned up his nose and ran his fingers through Sukenya's hair. "What have you done to your hair since last Saturday?" he asked in horror. "It hasn't even been a week Suk," he scolded. "Not even a week!"

"But don't worry," Jason laughed, "because by the time we're finished with you missy, everything will be back in place."

"Thanks to Nicole and Chris," Bobby smiled. "We are here for the duration of your wedding gurl, for the duration!"

Sukenya's evening of fun ended with a wonderful and pleasant surprise just as the ladies had anticipated.

Thirty

Today is Friday, she thought to herself, as she sat up in bed. *One day before my wedding. One more day before I am Mrs. Gregory Hollingsworth the third. This is my last day of being a single woman.*

Sukenya leaned over and pulled open the top right drawer of her nightstand. She then pulled out her journal and began to write.

Well, she wrote. *Here it is, my final day of being single. Tomorrow I will walk down the aisle and marry my one and only true love and soul mate, Mr. Gregory Hollingsworth III...*

Greg has made me see just how wonderful love can be. Through his unselfish love, he has taught me that true love doesn't hurt nor cause pain. For true love is the only love that accepts you just as you are. It doesn't compromise your feelings or your thoughts.

Instead true love enhances your very being within, blossoming like a delicate flower during the very beginning of spring.

True love gives you the faith to believe, to trust, and to cherish without doubt and without fear.

With love, all obstacles can be conquered. Through love, I was able to confront my pain, release my anger and bring closure to my past. Therefore I am now free. Free to love Greg with all of my heart. And I thank you God for revealing this to me and for giving me a second and honest chance at love.

Forever yours, Sukenya.

Sukenya closed her journal, softly kissed the cover and placed it back in her nightstand.

"Now if only Greg will give me a second chance after I tell him about St. Thomas," she sighed as she stretched out in her bed and snuggled back under her covers.

"But when? Tomorrow is supposed to be our wedding day."

"It's the only way," Sukenya cried as she unburdened her heart to her three friends later that morning. "In my heart, I now know that I love Greg fully and completely. I also know that if I want our marriage to truly be blessed by God we cannot begin our union with lies and secrets. I must tell Greg the truth!" she sighed. "But when?"

Sukenya pondered the entire day as to when and how to tell Greg about Austin. She knew she was taking a big risk. But Sukenya also knew it was a risk she had to take.

As friends and family arrived at her home to offer her well wishes and advice, Sukenya's only thought was Greg. As she received her facial, manicure, pedicure and full body massage, her only thought was Greg. As she soaked in a hot seaweed and honey bubble bath, her only thought was Greg.

Finally, at 12:30 am on Saturday, August 9th 2003, the day of Sukenya's and Greg's wedding, when in exactly fourteen hours, they were scheduled to exchange their wedding vows in front of over three hundred guests, Sukenya decided to call Greg!

Greg's cell phone began ringing at exactly 12:30 am right in the middle of his bachelor party. *Who could this be*, he thought as he pulled the phone out of his pocket. Greg recognized Sukenya's number on his caller ID and chuckled as he answered the phone.

"Sukenya I told you I was going to behave myself tonight," he laughed.

"Greg, I'm sorry to do this to you, but can you please meet me at your place?" Sukenya tearfully replied.

"Now?" he asked.

"Yes Greg," Sukenya cried. "This can't wait."

As Greg raced home. He could not imagine what could have Sukenya so upset. *Lord knows*, he thought, *I really do love this woman. How else can I explain leaving in the middle of my own Bachelor party?* He silently laughed while shaking his head back and forth.

Twenty minutes later, Greg was home. Greg walked into his five-bedroom home and found Sukenya sitting on the sofa staring into the fireplace. As Greg came closer, Sukenya looked up with tears streaming down her cheeks.

"Sukenya what's wrong baby?" a concerned Greg asked as he grabbed her cold hands and knelt down in front of her.

At first, Sukenya looked into Greg's eyes and then lowered her eyes in shame.

Finally, Sukenya took a deep breath and said, "Greg, I have to tell you something, but I don't know how to say it. I've been praying all day and searching for the right words to try and explain to you."

"Sukenya," Greg interrupted, "I love you with all of my heart and soul. There is nothing you can ever say or do to make me feel any differently."

Greg's words now made Sukenya's tears flow non stop.

"I... I... I love you too," she sobbed, "but I never really realized how much until I was in St. Thomas."

"St. Thomas?" a puzzled Greg asked.

"Yes," she cried, now trying to regain her composure. "Greg, while I was in St. Thomas, I ran into... Austin. I looked up one afternoon," she cried. "And there he was! After nine long years of nothing, there stood the man who first promised to love me forever. The man who promised to send for me once he became settled in California, the man who promised me the world, but instead, left me with a broken heart.

Greg, please believe me when I say. ... I don't know what happened. When I saw Austin, all the feelings I thought I had buried away so many years ago came rushing back without any warning. It was as if I had stepped back into time."

Sukenya told Greg about her entire time with Austin. She left nothing out.

She was in the process of telling Greg about their final night, when Greg interrupted her and asked as the clock struck 1:45 am. "Sukenya, do you still love him?"

"That's what I'm trying to tell you," she tearfully replied as her tears once again began to flow. "Greg," she cried, "when I saw Austin, and he kissed me, my

216

heart exploded with all of the feelings I thought I had buried away so many years ago. I later realized, those feelings that came rushing back were not feelings of love, but rather feelings of an unresolved past, a past that needed closure. During my final night in St Thomas, I realized the difference between wanting to be loved and truly being loved. I realized that night that all I ever wanted from Austin, was his unconditional love. The kind of love that he promised me so many years before, but never freely gave. What I also realized that night Greg, is all you've ever tried to do is love and accept me for who I am. You've never tried to change me and you never once tried to hurt me. You Greg, are the kind and gentle man I've longed for all of my adult life, but was too afraid to accept and love. And why?" Sukenya asked then answered, "because of an unresolved pain from my past! A past that came full circle and made me realize just how much I love and need you in my life Greg. You and only you!"

Greg stared at Sukenya for a moment, just as the clock struck 2:15 am he asked, "Did you sleep with him Sukenya?"

Sukenya looked up at Greg, took a deep breath and looked him directly into his eyes as she answered, "No... No Greg... I never slept with

Austin… Although, had he not repeated to me those same words he said nine years ago, I would have. That Greg was the closest we ever came to actually making love."

"While in St. Thomas right?" Greg asked.

"No," Sukenya softly replied. "I mean ever."
At first Greg seemed puzzled. He looked at Sukenya for a moment and then stared deep into her red watery eyes as her words clicked inside of his head.

"You mean…" Greg spelled out the words "E. V. E. R? Like in never?" he asked.

"Yes Greg," Sukenya answered. "That is exactly what I mean. Austin was my first love, but we never actually made love. We came close, I mean really close but it never happened, so we decided to wait until after we were married, but that never happened either."

Greg, now more curious than anything slowly said, "Sooo Sukenya. If you and Austin dated all through high school and college and you two never, ever made love, Does this mean…?"

He paused for a moment and rubbed his chin, which was Greg's way of really thinking. And then started his question again. "Does this mean…?" Now scratching his head, "Are you saying…?"

Sukenya knew what Greg was trying to ask her, so to help him along, she simply blurted out the answer. "Yes, Greg, yes. It means exactly what you are thinking. When you and I made love for the very first time, it was my first time."

Sukenya now half embarrassed and half proud said, "Greg, after Austin left, I literally shut down. I had no desire to be with anyone. And I sure as hell wasn't going to allow anyone to use my body for their own pleasure..."

As Sukenya continued talking, Greg thought back to the first time he and Sukenya attempted to make love. She was so nervous and uncomfortable they decided to cuddle instead, and ended up falling asleep in each other's arms. Sukenya and Greg spent their next three weeks sleeping together in this same manner. Without sex, just love and comfort. Greg loved Sukenya so much that he felt patient and content with simply waking up beside her. Then one morning, on a cold and snowy day, Sukenya and Greg made love for the first time.

"Greg?" Sukenya called out interrupting his thoughts as the clock struck 3:45 am "Are you listening to me?"

Greg stood up, and looked into Sukenya's eyes as he extended his right hand and motioned her to grab it. As she placed her left hand into his, he gently pulled her up off of the sofa and said, "Sukenya, God knew that in order for you to fully love me and begin our new lives together as husband and wife, you had to confront your pain, release your anger, and bring closure to your past."

Hey, she thought to herself. *Has this man been reading my journal?*

"Sukenya," an elated Greg smiled and said, "While you were in St. Thomas, you were able to do just that. Don't you get it?" he asked. "Don't you Sukenya? This!" he said loudly, now smiling with tears in his eyes, "has always been in the Master's plan!"

Greg picked up Sukenya and twirled her around and around and around until he became so dizzy they both fell on top of the sofa out of exhaustion.

As their breathing returned to normal, Greg looked into Sukenya's eyes and said, "It's not there anymore." He studied her eyes and moved closer towards Sukenya to get a better look and then repeated his words again. "It's not there anymore."

"What's not there?" Sukenya finally asked.

"The sadness in your eyes Sukenya," he answered, "the sadness in your eyes..."

"Sukenya baby, I knew from the beginning that there was something or someone who had caused you a great deal of pain. The kind of pain a person locks deep inside the deepest part of their heart. Never realizing how pain shows through your eyes, the only outward part of your body able to expose your soul. That was the part of you Sukenya I knew I didn't have, but believed that one day, in time, you would love and trust me enough to let me inside of that part of your heart and together erase all of your pain, and replace it with our love." Although," he laughed, "I never imagined it would happen on our wedding day!"

"Greg," Sukenya nervously asked as she looked at the clock, which read 4:45 am, "Does this mean we're still getting married?"

"Sukenya," Greg replied, "I told you in the beginning, there was nothing you could ever say or ever do to make me stop loving you. And right now Sukenya, at this very moment, I love you more than I could have ever imagined! Sukenya my love," he softly whispered. "You have exposed the most intimate part of your soul to me."

"That's because, you are the man I've longed for all of my adult life. You, Greg, are my lover, and my protector, my joy and my companion. You, dear sweet Greg are my true love and soul mate!"

The two embraced and kissed. But for the first time since meeting, they kissed without any barriers between them, just love.

Finally Sukenya pulled away and said, "Thank you Greg, thank you for believing in me."

"Always, Sukenya," he laughed. "Always."

It was now 5:00 Saturday morning. In nine hours, Sukenya and Greg would become husband and wife.

Thirty One

As Greg drove Sukenya home, she quietly thought to herself, *Today is Saturday, August 9th 2003. Our wedding day. A day filled with love, excitement and honor. A day filled with promise and determination. Determination to be forever and ever Amen.*

"Greg, I could have driven home," Sukenya laughed as they rode in his car.

"Nah that's all right," Greg replied as he pulled up in front of Sukenya's home. "By me dropping you off, I now have peace of mind knowing you made it home safely."

Greg then stepped out of his car and walked around to the passenger side where Sukenya patiently waited. As he grabbed the passenger side handle and opened the door, he continued his conversation. "Because, in seven hours my love, all I want to see is my beautiful bride walking down the aisle."

Sukenya laughed as Greg took her by the hand and helped her out of his car.

"Actually it's six hours and forty five minutes," she said.

"Not soon enough," he laughed. "Not soon enough." Greg walked Sukenya to her front door, gave her a quick peck on the lips and playfully walked back to his car. As Greg pulled off he yelled, "I love you Sukenya! See you at two..."

Sukenya grabbed her heart and shook her head as she waved good-bye and walked through the front door of her home.

"Thank you Jesus," she softly whispered as she walked towards her bedroom. "Thank you for helping us make it to this wonderful and blessed day!"

"Sukenya!" yelled her Great Aunt Cassie as she walked out of the bathroom half startling her. "Girl, didn't your mother teach you anything?" she jokingly asked. "Why on earth would a man want to buy the cow if she's willing to give the milk away for free?"

"Oh Aunt Cassie," Sukenya laughed and whispered as she helped her back into bed. "It's not what you're thinking. Greg and I just had some last minute details to work out. That's all. Besides, this cow is getting married today!"

Sukenya laughed as she kissed her great aunt on the forehead and headed out of the bedroom.

"Not if your hair isn't right," scolded Ty as he met Sukenya coming out of the room.

"Where have you been gurl?" he asked as they walked towards the kitchen. "I mean poor KiKi has been frantic with worry."

"Oh Ty," she laughed. "It's okay! I'm here now!"

"Good morning Sukenya," her mother smiled as she sat at the kitchen table drinking a hot cup of coffee.

"Good Morning Mom," Sukenya replied as she pulled out a chair to sit down.

"Sukenya!" her mother cheerfully squealed as she placed her right hand on the right side of her face. "My God baby, look at you! At this very moment, you do not need a stitch of makeup on your beautiful face."

"That's because the glow you have right now Sukenya," KiKi teased as he entered the kitchen, "is as bright as the Sun! Gurl you're so bright you're giving me a sunburn! And Sukenya, my lady, I think it is time for you to start getting dressed."

"Well, Sir," she teased in a British like accent. "Please let us begin this miracle transformation!"

For the next three hours, they all laughed as KiKi and Ty primped and combed and flossed and brushed and tugged and pulled until voilà! There stood Sukenya, fully dressed, a natural beauty in her own right, for she was stunning, absolutely stunning. KiKi and Ty were so overwhelmed, they cried with joy!

"You're beautiful Sukenya," her family beamed. "Simply beautiful."

After a morning photo session with her bridesmaids, Sukenya's limo pulled up to the church at exactly 12:30 pm. As she stepped out of the limo, she was greeted by friends and family members who wanted to get a quick peek at the bride before the ceremony.

"Oh she's so beautiful," they all agreed.

Sukenya felt as if she was floating on air. "If heaven is anything like how I'm feeling right now," she smiled, as she walked up the stairs of the church, "then it is going to be the most amazing place to live one day."

"Aunty Suk! Aunty Suk!" yelled Brandy's two beautiful daughters Brittany and Chloe as they ran up to Sukenya shouting with excitement, "Our dresses look just like yours. And look at our shoes Aunty Suk! Look! Aunty Nicole had our shoes made in Italy," they giggled.

"Oh really?" Sukenya laughed.

"Well my shoes look just like my two beautiful flower girls," she laughed as she lifted her dress high enough to expose her shoes to the girls.

"Mommy, Mommy!" the two girls screamed with excitement. "Aunty Suk has shoes like ours, and we have dresses like her dress. Are we getting married today too Mommy?" they asked with huge smiles and bright eyes. "Are we?"

"You girls don't want to give your mother a heart attack do you?" Alexandria laughed as she walked towards them.

"Aaah! It's Aunty Alex!" the girls screamed as they ran towards her.

"Guess what Aunty Alex, guess what? We're getting married today!" they giggled. "We're getting married with Aunty Suk! See our dresses?" they asked as they twirled around and around.

"Oh they're beautiful," Alexandria laughed, "simply beautiful! But listen girls, we have to be really quiet when we go inside the church OK?" she asked.

"Okay Aunty Alex. Aunty, will you hold our hands?" the girls asked.

"Well of course I will."

"Can we skip a little?"

"Only to the front of the door. Then we will quietly walk down the hall to the room where your mother and Aunty Suk are waiting until the ceremony begins. Ok girls?"

"Okay Aunty!"

Alexandria and the children entered the church and walked into the room where Sukenya and Brandy were patiently waiting. They arrived just in time to see Sukenya turning around to show Brandy how wonderful the sapphire and diamond tear drop necklace looked around her throat. Sukenya caught a glimpse of Alexandria entering the room with the children and laughed. "Well isn't this a sight. Alexandria with children!"

"With all that has happened this year," Nicole said as she entered the room. "The thought of Alexandria with children would be better than the sweetest icing on any cake!"

"After you my dear cousin," Alexandria laughed in a dry tone and repeated, "after you."

The women all laughed, and then turned their attention back to Sukenya who, was glowing in love. The three friends stood and admired Sukenya while attempting to keep their tears from overflowing.

"Let's not do this!" Sukenya tearfully begged. "Because if one starts we're going to need a mop and a bucket to wipe up all of our tears."

"Sukenya, only you would think of a mop and a bucket on your wedding day! Damn Girl, you are such a Cinderella!" Alexandria playfully squawked.

The four women cracked up laughing before they were able to shed tears of joy.

It was now 1:45 pm. As latecomers made a mad dash into the church in an attempt to try and find a seat before the ceremony began, Rever the wedding coordinator poked her head into the room where Sukenya and her wedding party were enthusiastically waiting. "Ladies," she said, "it's time to line up."

The women looked at the coordinator and laughed wildly as they said in harmony,

"We haven't heard anyone say that to us since our days at Norfolk State some twenty years ago, when we were on line together and pledged Delta Sigma Theta."

"The only difference now," Brandy laughed, "is today Sukenya, instead of you being first on line, you're going to be fourth on line."

"Only until after the ceremony," Alexandria joked.

"Isn't that right Yoda?" Nicole teased. *"Yoda"* was the line name Sukenya had been given by her then big sisters, or actual members of the sorority during a time in which the women pledged, a process known to them as *'being on line.'*... Being connected to a group of girls for a set period of time while working together as a team and learning the history of their sorority before actually being accepted. That is, making it to the final ceremony. A ceremony fondly known as *'crossing over.'*

The coordinator clearly didn't get the joke.

But the four friends of many years laughed hysterically as they remembered their days of yesteryear...

The doors opened at exactly 2:00 pm. Beautiful and seductive Alexandria was the first to enter. Her very distinctive looks overshadowed her purest quality, that is, the ability to be funny yet extremely shrewd. She had sought out and found the enemy who had unsuccessfully tried to destroy what she considered a part of her.

Through her detective work, she also discovered her enemy's disloyalty to his own wife. By having a secret vasectomy before he and his wife were married. It was his twisted way of making sure he'd never have to share any of her money.

"*That was before he met up with Chris and Sanjay,*" Alexandria silently laughed as she began her walk down the aisle. "*Once Chris informed Sanjay of Sam's wicked ways, Sanjay paid Sam a visit and made him an offer he could not refuse. Sam's life for Sintech. After all, Sintech was Sanjay's baby.*

As a show of humility Sam agreed to give Sanjay Triscope as well... Yeah right," Alexandria smiled. "*Sam did whatever he could, not to make Sanjay retaliate even further by raiding his wife's entire empire and thereby exposing Sam for the coward that he was. It is amazing what a man who owns enough oil to fill the entire state of New Jersey can do with a man like Sam. Best of all, Sanjay gave Nicole the entire company! Talk about sweet revenge,*" she giggled as she glided to her place.

As Alexandria settled in, she glanced over and smiled at James, her one and only true love and soul mate and quickly said to herself. "*Brandy, I sure hope you know what you're talking about with this crackers and ginger ale remedy because I don't know if I can take this queasy feeling for the entire nine months. But,*" she smiled, "*just knowing the look in James eyes when he sees our baby for the very first time is well worth it!*"

Next to enter was Nicole who was absolutely stunning. Gifted with brains as well as beauty, her mere presence demanded attention. The computer wiz had triumphantly survived treachery and deceit. And in the process, found a true friend and confidante to help keep her balanced.

Sukenya and Greg were truly made for each other, she thought as she proceeded down the aisle. *Shoot,* she smiled, as she glanced over at Chris standing so handsomely next to James. *The same could be said for Chris and I. Because,* she smiled as she took her place next to Alexandria, *the brother is fine! Besides, Sanjay did say he was mine exclusively!*

As Brandy entered, she was absolutely beautiful. Beautiful in a way that said, "Hello world here I am!" Head up, back straight and eyes straight ahead. Except today, as she walked towards the front of the church, she took a quick glance at her true love and soul mate, Darius, who, was standing so handsomely next to Greg.

Brandy gave Darius a quick wink as she thought to herself, *Oh lord, why did I let Alexandria talk me into wearing a pasty bra with a fake left breast in it. I sure hope it's not crooked,* she smiled as she gracefully took her place in front of Alexandria. Then promptly laughed and quietly said, "oh well at least today, I have cleavage."

Jason and Bobby had the honor or rolling down the white runner for Sukenya.

When their task was complete, they looked at each other and said, "Perfect. Simply perfect."

Brandy's beautiful daughters entered next, delicately throwing flowers on the runner just as they had rehearsed. Every now and then, the girls would stop, giggle, wave, and say "hello" to people they knew.

"Hi Grandma and Pop-Pop, see our dresses? Hi Mommy and Daddy, are you all getting married today too?" they asked with excitement. "Daddy, where are Miles and Brandon's rings for their ring pillows?"

"Out of the mouths of babes," the guests chuckled. "Out of the mouths of babes."

"Are you ready Baby?" Sukenya's father asked in a loving fatherly tone, as he gently lowered his daughter's wedding veil.

"Yes Daddy," she answered. "I am finally ready!"

In their final attempt to keep Sukenya as perfect and as beautiful as she was, KiKi and Ty fluffed out the back of Sukenya's beautiful bell shaped, sleeveless, form fitting, corset-designed gown.

Her 12 foot Egyptian silk train stretched clear across the hall, displaying the skillfully embroidered cross with the initials GH and SH on each side.

Once KiKi and Ty performed their final inspection, they raised their hands just as the clock struck 2:30 and said, "Marvelous Sukenya, simply marvelous."

KiKi then handed Sukenya, who is one of the top female African American news anchorwoman in the country, a microphone. Sukenya tearfully smiled as she thanked KiKi and began to recite over the church's intercom, for all to hear, a very special poem she'd written as her surprise wedding day gift to Greg.

Sukenya began her surprise by saying,

"Greg, as you stand at the alter with anticipation to see,
You will hear the soft words of your bride to be.
It is clear to me and I do understand,
That God has truly blessed me,
With a loving and spiritual man.
Our love will be built on a solid foundation,
Consisting of trust, respect and above all, communication.

Now as I walk to you in the arms of my father,
I'll never need to look any further,
For you my love have helped me to see,
That God has truly delivered you to me.
And as the doors open and our hearts beat as one,
I dedicate to you my love, this most deserving song."

As Sukenya's very special song entitled *"God's Greatest Gift"* began to play, KiKi and Ty opened the double doors. The guests stood and gasped with admiration as they looked upon Sukenya and her father standing in the doorway of the vestibule. For Sukenya's appearance was truly one of exquisité beauty.

Greg's watery eyes focused on his beautiful bride as his heart skipped a beat while Sukenya's song played in the background. At that precise moment he quietly said to himself, "I feel nothing but pure and honest joy in my heart today Lord, and I thank you for that. Because, there standing in the entrance is the woman I fell in love with the first time I laid eyes on her.

There standing in the entrance is the woman other guys once teased me about for trying so hard.

There stands Sukenya, a natural beauty... my natural beauty... my love... my life...my soul mate! And I thank you for blessing me to truly know and understand all that she is. A gift," he quietly said. "A wonderful and beautiful gift. God's greatest gift... to me. That I shall love, honor, respect and cherish always, till death do us part. This I promise today and always..."

"I love you Daddy," Sukenya whispered to her father as she began her graceful walk down the aisle.

"I love you too baby," he whispered as he and his daughter walked arm and arm towards the one and only true love of her life, Mr. Gregory Hollingsworth III.

Sukenya's eyes scanned the room as she gracefully smiled and nodded at her guests while slowly strolling down the aisle. As she came closer towards the front, her eyes met Brandy's, Nicole's and Alexandria's. Sukenya remembered all that they had gone through since meeting in college some 20 years ago as silly freshmen. Now today, they were in their own right indeed: *True Women* of *Substance*. Sukenya's father, however, interrupted her thoughts as he gently placed his daughter's hand on top of Greg's and humbly stepped to the side.

As Sukenya gazed into Greg's eyes, she quietly thought, *"Yes Lord!* Here stands my Prince Charming... My true love... My soul mate! A Man that I shall love, honor, respect and cherish always, till death do us part... This I promise today and always..."

However, for a split second, Sukenya turned and looked back at her three smiling *'sisters'*
and continued her original thought, which ended with:

During a span of 20 years, through God's grace and mercy, we've faced and battled infertility, cancer, deceit and betrayal... Only to triumphantly rise together with a bond, stronger and better than ever! In the name of Sisterhood!!!

"Dearly Beloved..."

The End

In The Name of Sisterhood

Last Minute Thoughts From The Author

Hello, I hope you have enjoyed reading my first novel entitled, *In the Name of Sisterhood.*

While this story is fiction, I'm sure that it could very well be someone's story. My hope is that you will walk away feeling empowered to go after your dreams with a vengeance, especially those of you who are at the starting gate of life. Strive to succeed and to not just get by... Know all that you do today will follow you for the rest of your life. Be the person at the top always looking up and not the person at the bottom always looking down. For like a bucket of crabs, those who see you looking down will always try to pull and keep you down.

Learn and understand that life is about learning, and about making mistakes. The key is to realize your mistakes, move on, and not tarry long, for none of us are perfect. Always remember Jesus Christ is the only perfect man who has ever walked this earth. He forgave us, so learn to forgive your self.

Have faith, courage and determination. Be happy in life, stay focused and remember to always pray so that one day, when all is quiet, you'll be able to look back twenty, thirty, or fifty plus years later and be proud of yourself and all of your accomplishments.

Embrace your true friends and understand their purpose in your life. For while they may not always be around, something about them will stay with you forever...

Let your legacy be one of honor and not one of disgrace. Know that you are the author, director and star of your own story. How it ends depends on you... For God gave you the ability to think and to decide, to choose and to make choices, to believe and to know.

Thank you!

In The Name of Sisterhood
Order Form

Use this convenient form to order additional
copies of
In The Name of Sisterhood

Purchaser Information (Please Print):

Name: _____

Address: _____

City: _____ **State:** _____

Zip Code: _____

Phone: (   ) _____

_____ Copies of book @ $14.95 each $ _____
Postage and handling @ $7.00 per book $ _____
New Jersey residents add .90 tax per book $ _____
Total amount enclosed $ _____

Send Checks or Money Orders to:

Phyllis Simms

c/o Cross House Publishing
P.O. Box 703
Burlington, NJ 08016

Visit our website at:
www.crosshousepublishing.com

Thank you for your support!